S E S S I O N
9

THE OFFICIAL NOVELIZATION

CHRISTIAN FRANCIS
BASED ON THE SCREENPLAY BY
BRAD ANDERSON & STEPHEN GEVEDON

For Vicky x

978-1-916582-59-0 (eBook)
978-1-916582-60-6 (Trade Paperback)
978-1-916582-61-3 (Jacketed Hardcover)
978-1-916582-62-0 (Mass Market Paperback)

Contents

How It Came To Be

Brad Anderson

The normal process when you make a film is to write a script set in a location and later, once you have begun prepping the film, scout out a real location that matches as close as possible what you have written. In other words, you try to match reality to your imagination. With my movie *Session 9* this process was reversed.

I first saw Danvers back in the early 90's when I lived in Boston and would occasionally drive by it on the way to Maine. As you'd speed North on Route 1 you'd see the ominous jag of its spires and copper towers rising up out of the dark tree-line. I was always struck by how bizarre this sight was—this 19th century brick and granite Asylum, something straight out of Dickens or Poe, looming up on that hill overlooking Honda dealerships, neon strip clubs and cheesy family restaurants. It was a sight that beckoned you closer.

I finally did get closer when I helped out on a film

(*The Crucible*, appropriately enough) that was using the buildings, at least the ones that were still safe, as production facilities. At the time the state of Massachusetts offered abandoned hospitals like Danvers and Met State to movie companies free of charge as a way to lure more Hollywood films to the Boston area. A strange kind of lure no doubt, but it worked. And frankly, who better to "commit themselves" to old asylums then those from the undoubtedly insane world of show business.

Anyhow, I was able to explore a bit at that time. I was fascinated by the hugeness of the place, the lurid, almost sinister contrast between it's lovely pastoral setting - the orchards, the meadows, the garden paths - and the terrifying aspect of the hospital itself - it's sharp slate roofs, caged in windows, **WARNING: DO NOT ENTER** stickers plastered on nearly every door.

An idea began to germinate - why simply use the hospital as a production facility? Why not use the hospital as a movie location? Set a story here. Tailor a story for this place and shoot it here. The advantages immediately became clear to me...

First, and maybe most important, it would be free. One spectacular location, no charge. That would go down well with the financiers. Two, it would be convenient. We could shoot in just one location where we could also set up our production offices. In essence we could make the Danvers complex into our own back lot - the Hospital becomes the set, annex buildings serve as offices, catering, wardrobe, etc. One stop shopping. Third, no one had really done it before. So it seemed like a mildly original idea.

So in 2000, about six years after that initial brain storm, along with my writing partner Steve Gevedon, I began formulating a story that could be set in this single remarkable location. It was then we discovered the fourth advantage of shooting at Danvers - it is a place rife with stories. Larger than life stories. Heroic stories. Spooky stories. Tragic stories. We pulled many ideas for our screenplay from these stories, from what we read on line, from people we spoke with, ex patients, doctors, nurses.

About midway through writing we realized we needed to see the place again. Steve had never been there, I hadn't been there in years and we were working off my memories of the place.

The problem was we didn't want to go there on an official film scout. I knew the state film officials would probably discourage us from shooting there at all. Danvers was disintegrating fast. In the five years since I had first wandered its corridors and tunnels, floors and ceilings had collapsed, windows had been smashed, oak-paneled rooms had been vandalized. Asbestos hung in flaky chunks off every pipe. Many areas we were told were entirely off limits because they were too dangerous.

So we decided to sneak in.

I had recently discovered some websites created by fans of "urban spelunking". These are "thrill junkies" - of a sort - who break into abandoned buildings, subway tunnels and old hospitals. They take photos, explore and write about it on their websites. I learned one group had a trip planned to Danvers so in early Spring Steve and I joined them.

We parked behind a mini mall near Danvers and set off through the woods up the hill upon which the hospital sits. We were decked out like a navy seal team, dark clothes, backpacks, flashlights. Even walkie talkies. We moved fast, keeping low to avoid being spotted by the security guards that roam the grounds.

We rapidly crossed a large meadow. Our group leader informed us we were walking over the grave sites of hundreds of patients who had died anonymously at Danvers over the past 150 years, An auspicious start. At the treeline we stopped. There was the main Hospital building, surrounded by rusty lamp posts and numerous trees, all dead.

We were guided to a more modern side building. They jimmied open a rusty door. We were inside. I looked out a broken window and wondered how we were going to get over to the older main building, 200 yards away, without crossing the huge lawn and totally exposing ourselves to the guards. The guide chuckled. He led us down...to the basement.

Rusty gurneys, scary looking medical equipment, moldy boxes of Saltines, gauze bandages and canned peaches - Danvers was a fallout shelter for the local community up until a few years ago. It was cold in the basement. Abnormally cold. We could see our breath in the beams of our flashlights. Suddenly we were in a narrow tunnel. On the floor were painted arrows pointing towards WARD A. That didn't sound promising. This was one of dozens of tunnels that connect the buildings of Danvers. Food, supplies, patients would be wheeled through these tunnels on cold winter nights. We were walking fast. No one spoke. It seemed to take us too long to get to the other side. When we did finally pop out into a larger tunnel our guide told us we had just crossed all the way over to the main building. We laughed, thrilled. It felt like we were in enemy territory now.

We silently climbed a stairwell bisected by a high metal fence, once used to separate the more unruly patients from the staff. And then we were stepping into the long corridor of WARD A. Off to each side were dozens of small rooms, cells really, with barred windows and thick wooden doors. These were seclusions. The patients rooms. I stepped into one.

The walls were covered with old magazine cut outs, images of mountains, puppies, Richard Nixon, flowers, a kitchen stove. Images that had meaning to someone once. On the floor was a pigeon skeleton, perfectly intact, bleached white by time and the sun. It had flown in a broken window and gotten lost and had somehow ended up in this small room and died.

Wow.

This place was filmmakers dream. Or nightmare. I

Brad Anderson

knew then we would have more then enough ideas and images to write into a dozen screenplays. The group leader was calling out. It was time to take us to the old surgery room, where they allegedly performed lobotomies in the 1950's...

Before I stepped out of the seclusion I put a hand to the wall of the seclusion. Feeling it. A sadness overwhelmed me. So much sadness here. So many lives halted. Months later our lead actor Peter Mullan would relate having the same experience when we were shooting *Session 9* here. He admitted to me that between takes he would often place his ear against the walls. And somehow they spoke. Of the dramas. Of the tragedies. Of the loneliness of the countless lives that passed through here. He said this sensation informed his performance in the film. I believe it. Danvers is that kind of a place. It tells its story, a cautionary tale, to those who will listen.

Prologue

From the darkened kitchen of the Hobbes household, eerie strains of The Platters echoed from a crackling radio, drifting through each silent room and seeping into the deepest shadows.

Festive cheer that had been tainting the airwaves since November had paused, replaced by haunting strings and piano notes creeping through the house, coiling in the dark like a sinister menace. In the living room, lights from an artificial Christmas tree flickered with an unnerving yellow and white glow. They cast ominously distorted shadows that danced across the walls in a grotesque pantomime. A pine scent mixed with a faint, unsettling odor of something metallic. Something sour.

Mary Hobbes, dressed in her nightie, sat cross-legged on the living room rug, holding a brand-new doll. At eleven years old, she should have been excited about the presents wrapped under the tree in front of her. Yet only one had been opened, its paper splayed across the floor, torn open and discarded. On the rug beside her lay her doll's head, pulled from the body she held lovingly.

"What happened to her head?" Mary muttered, in a kindly, childlike tone.

"Danny pulled it off!" she replied to herself in a raspy voice.

"My goodness. Why would he do such a terrible thing?"

"'Cos Danny's a meanie," she spat.

A giggle escaped her lips as she sat in the dark room, amusing. Her eyes, though, usually bright and lively, gleamed with a disconcerting intensity.

"It's all okay now," her soft voice said. "Danny can't hurt you."

Mary then cried in silence.

She did not know how long it had been between that night and the appearance of Ernie Rivett, the next-door neighbor. All she knew was that the usual barrage of festive tunes took over the song that had been playing.

"Hello?" an old man called from the open front door.

As he took a tentative step into the hallway, a pang of concern struck Ernie Rivett. Sure, folk from Lowell sometimes left their houses unlocked, he mused, but they wouldn't leave their front door wide open in the dead of night. Nor have the radio blaring for hours.

"What the hell is going on here?" he grumbled, heart pounding.

Ernie had known the Hobbes family for years— Frank and Nancy were good people, just inconsiderate when drinking was involved in their fun.

But this seemed different.

There were no cheers of celebration. No evidence anyone was even here.

His mind raced with possibilities, each more sinister than the last. Had there been a break-in? An accident?

He gulped, the fear bitter in his mouth.

He wasn't young anymore, and his nerves weren't what they used to be. But he had to find out what was going on. Especially since Ernie's wife had begged him over two hours prior to get the noise shut off. And he could tell this was not the drunken musical escapade his wife had thought. No one was here, yet Ernie felt like something was watching him from the darkness.

Chilled winter air swept through the doorframe and past Ernie. The stinging cold, far worse than outside, forced his teeth to chatter quietly. He zipped his coat up further over his pajamas.

"Frank? Nancy?" he called with a trembling voice. "Anyone home?"

His mind raced with images of encountering an armed intruder in the middle of ransacking. He should leave, he told himself.

Flashlight in hand, he shone it ahead, walking with

trepidation toward the living room but ready to bolt at any given moment. "You better be drunk, Frank." Ernie sighed.

A useless beginning to a featherweight threat. Being almost eighty, he had no real fight in him nor any pull to start an argument.

As Ernie swung his flashlight around the corner, shining it through the open double doorway into the living room, he gasped. With his heart thudding, he stepped back, jolting at Mary's presence, who sat facing away from him. Almost on cue, the song on the radio then stopped, replaced by inaudible chatter from the DJ.

"That you, Mary?" Ernie whispered, stepping forward.

Still turned away, Mary just carried on, looking down at the headless doll in her hand, weeping.

"D'you know where your folks are, dear?" He came closer. "Are you crying?"

As soon as those three words were uttered, he knew for sure that things here were pretty far from okay. As he approached, he quietly wondered why her normal light-red hair was so dark in this light and why her nightie looked black.

Tiptoeing around her, Ernie shone the flashlight down upon the young child. It was only when the beam illuminated her face that Ernie Rivett was pulled into an unwelcome, terrifying reality.

Ernie stared, his mouth agape. He saw that her

nightie was not black but bathed in crimson. Her arms and legs were the same, slathered in dried blood.

Before this old man could react, Mary snapped her head toward him. Tears no longer falling. Caught in the flashlight's bright gleam, a wide insidious grin crept over her blood-spattered face.

Chapter 1

The Bughouse

The Danvers State Hospital, once known as the Danvers Insane Asylum, had stood abandoned on the west side of town, high up on the hill, for almost a decade. Even before its closure, rumors and urban legends had run rampant, not only through the town but through the whole state itself. Tales of the building's deteriorating condition from many years of neglect, of medical abuse and malpractice within its walls. Tales of cruelty. Tales of horror. All told in excitable, gossiped whispers, many devoid of firsthand facts.

The Danvers State Hospital had become a boogeyman for the locals. A place where someone often knew someone else who had once met a person who saw something happen there. A place where tales of ghostly happenings within the hospital's expansive complex were told over late-night drinks in the seediest of dive bars.

It was a place that most sane people inherently knew to stay away from. The same as they had done since it had opened its doors in 1878.

The Bughouse, that is what the locals in Danvers had colloquially referred to the hospital as for the best part of a century.

You better, or it's the Bughouse for ya! was a phrase parents would harmlessly threaten their children with if they stepped out of line.

This kind of threat became more sinister, as the town had to welcome ex-patients who had been released from that hospital. Patients who walked through the town in a vacant daze, each bereft of any personality beyond their unnaturally pliable blankness. Products of "mental quelling," of "surgical silence," as the professionals had dubbed lobotomies.

You better, or it's the Bughouse for ya! soon morphed into *You better, or the Bughouse ghouls'll get ya!*

Children through the generations had spun tales of bloodthirsty monsters born from the hospital's medical horrors. Lobotomized shells of people turned zombies who craved brains to feast upon—a schoolyard joke, sure, but one the younger kids took quite seriously.

Since it had first opened, it presented itself with a veneer of caring and community. Its Gothic build, constructed according to a typical Kirkbride plan, with wings stretching out from the main central house, impressed all who visited.

The interiors were, at first, no different in their impressiveness, with walls adorned with decorative plaster moldings beneath large chandeliers and tin ceilings.

The hospital seemed almost like a manor that belonged to some rich aristocrat. But what this building was built for was masked in the construction's little details; the inner walls were mostly curved, with few pointed edges, all for patients' safety. Images of dahlias could also be found engraved on stone and metalwork throughout the grounds, as well as photos of the building itself.

This flower brings a symbol of new beginnings, a fact the staff were eager to mention. Over time, as stories spread about the horrors within its walls, these flowers, with their hopeful ideology, changed. With no color to these dahlias, aside from the dark metal and stone they were carved on, they seemed more like black dahlias, which symbolized an entirely different meaning: sadness and betrayal. Something that, over time, became a more fitting emblem of the hospital's grim history.

Starting as a caring facility, with staff dedicated to a patient's well-being, the hospital even welcomed guests.

Expansive gardens behind the complex boasted opulent flower beds and sculpted hedgerows, drawing thousands of visitors through its large metal gates. Each of them drawn to the beauty of the buildings and grounds as an impressive curio.

Not to see only the grounds, visitors sometimes arrived wanting to see the insane up close and personal. Using the gardens to mask their macabre fascination. And patients were often seated in wheelchairs throughout the shrubbery, on display for anyone to gawk at, a reminder to visitors of the hospital's purpose.

Often, to assuage their guilt, visitors would bring gifts—knitted blankets, bottles of perfume, trinkets that were useless to the patients—eagerly accepted by the staff, who would take them home for themselves. The patients not deemed worthy enough.

Then, in the 1950s, the advent of psychopharmaceuticals and new surgical therapies emerged as cutting-edge cures for mental health—treatments the hospital adopted enthusiastically. These new approaches were less convalescent and more immediate in their apparent curing, meaning patients could be treated and released at a much quicker rate.

Within the minds of the administrators, Danvers was a bastion for the three P's: Profit. Profit. Profit. They saw their adoption of newer care methodologies as essential to not only streamline the care versus cost process but to stand them ahead of the other more antiquated care facilities, which, in turn, had no choice but to follow suit.

From Westin Hills, Ohio, to Arkham, Massachusetts, the model of care Danvers had set was seen as the future.

But this future was one where the patient was not part of the equation, where care was just irrelevant.

With these new approaches to mental health medicine also came a vast new influx of funding from the state. More patients they took on to cure meant more money.

But the hospital got greedy, and patient numbers swelled, with too many to cure and turn around. Doubling, tripling, quadrupling the intended maximum, bringing in more and more money, money that flowed into the coffers of the administrators and senior doctors, not into the building's upkeep or medicine used.

Soon, whispers of the severe overcrowding, declining conditions intensified, as did the multiple stories of abuse.

Electroshock therapy and invasive psychosurgery became one-size-fits-all solutions for noncompliant patients for the sake of ease. If electroshock couldn't quell the mania, a full-frontal lobotomy was the next course of action. This savagery removed any trace of personality and led to the eventual patient's release without any proper care.

This hushed talk of the barbarism intensified over time, with the hospital becoming more feared than any prison in the area. If a person were labeled insane by the judicial system, they would often be sent to the Danvers State Hospital to be cured for their criminally mental maladies—no matter the perpetrator's age.

Children were as eagerly welcomed as adults within

their cruel walls. Year on year, with the rising influx of medical inmates, the staff soon became jailers, and the murderers were housed along with the infirm, each and all treated the same. As less than animals.

What once was a hospital had become a de facto criminal asylum. One which maintained order through abuse. Patients, if not drugged or mutilated, were abandoned in their cells without food or water. Overwhelmed orderlies, outnumbering medical staff, resorted to cruelty and fear to maintain their stronghold.

By the '80s, this once-caring facility had become a pit where the ill went to be drugged, cut into, then forgotten about. And state officials were unable to turn a blind eye to it anymore.

Over the subsequent decade, the hospital's operations were forced to wind down, with patients transferring to other institutions or being released back into the population.

In the summer of '92, the doors to this decayed, unkempt complex closed for good.

Over the subsequent years, the Danvers State Hospital stood untouched, further rotting into its foundations. A haunting specter for the community. Laying on the edge of town in a quiet malevolence. A sleeping beast no one dared confront.

As it stood empty, this abandoned monolith attracted mainly looters and vandals. Those who picked through the remnants of the building's stripped corpse and graffitied the walls.

But also, occasionally, children from the schools would break in. On a dare, these kids would only stay a short time, as it would not take long before they fearfully ran home, convinced that ghosts of abused patients still roamed the halls seeking revenge.

It may have been built to be a beacon of enlightened care, but the Danvers State Hospital had twisted into a terrifying monster, even in its current dormant, derelict state. Its very presence sent shivers down the spines of those who spoke of it. Telling their tales in hushed, fearful tones.

In the recesses of the state hospital's third-floor, a dark fungal growth climbed up the damp, cracked walls. This mold grew unabated in the dilapidation, latching onto anything it could reach.

Down the long corridor, with open rooms structured on both sides, slivers of moonlight shone through the doorways. This brightness, within the lens of the room's murky windows, transformed the light into a dull brownish hue that gave everything a dirtier, more squalid appearance. In this corridor, this dirty illumination caught dust particles that twirled down from the ceiling. Its plaster, on the verge of caving in on itself, was adorned with multitudes of small spiderweb-like cracks, each exposing the rotten roof beams.

This corridor, this building, this whole complex was dead and rotten.

On the floor, left like trash, lay pages of old medical files. Separated from their folders and barely readable from fading over time. They resembled leaves from trees that lay on the woodland ground, discarded evidence of what was once a verdant life.

At the end of the corridor, leading onto the next wing sat an old restraint chair with worn leather straps, blocking any further passage. Beyond it, in the deep shadows, a dark figure scuttled from one room to another.

Staring through his van's windshield, looking at the greenness of a meadow beyond a metal gate, Gordon Fleming was tired. At only forty years old, he felt as if he was somehow mistaken and was, in fact, double that age. As if, during his life, he had lived two years for every one and sat here at eighty, with the pains that came with that era. His bones ached, his muscles ached, and even his teeth felt sore. The heaviness of his eyelids pressed down, willing him to sleep. Even his shoulders sagged more than they ever had done before, as if the literal weight of the world was finally becoming insurmountable.

In his hands, he cradled a paper cup of warm black coffee. The kind he had every morning to push himself forward into the day. Yet, even after decades of drinking the stuff, he still hated its taste. He couldn't abide the bitterness but felt that he must have been wrong for that opinion. So, he drank it without complaint, more out of what he felt should've been a habit.

He thought his gray overalls felt tight on him, as if he had put on weight or that the clothes had shrunk in the wash. Yet he was thinner than he ever had been before, and these had not been washed since the last job— something he had meant to do but hadn't had the mental capacity to get done. He felt lucky it didn't stink.

From the speakers affixed in the van doors, voices from a talk radio show blared tinnily in the background.

Gordon, caught up in his own exhaustion, did not listen to what was being said and only heard a polyphony of disconnected phrases. *And how old were you when she drowned? All the sinners deserve to fry in the electric chair. So sick of left-wing tree huggers. No, she likes the top! Why? Because she's a freakin' control freak is why.* These voices said nothing to him nor meant anything. They just painted the background with a low-quality collage of noise.

For a second, as the radio continued with its banal opinions, he stared out from the driver's seat and mused silently, *I used to feel good, didn't I?*

Taking a deep breath in, he could not help but let out a loud, labored sigh.

"Fuckin' talk radio," a male voice said with a scoff from the passenger seat.

Gordon did not hear and remained staring vacantly ahead. He did not even notice the passenger had changed the radio channel and rested on a music station.

"That's more like it!" the voice said again.

Gordon dropped his gaze into the black liquid in his hands. The black coffee he hated. Yet, like always, he raised the cup and took a large gulp.

"Man, Gordo," the passenger said, "you look so beat. Sure you're up for this?"

Gordon, hearing the question, turned to look at his friend.

Phil Maddow, dressed in matching overalls—but in much better condition than Gordon's—was a sweet-looking thirty-five-year-old.

He furrowed his large hairy brows with genuine concern. "Was it your turn to feed Emma again?"

Forcing a weak smile, Gordon shook his head almost imperceptibly. "Nah," he said, low and gravelly. "Still got that ear infection, keeping us up at all hours."

"Still?" Phil's eyes widened with surprise. "God, she had that at the christening, right? How long's that been?"

Gordon took another sip from his cup.

"How's Wendy holding up with it all?" Phil asked.

Cracking his sore neck, Gordon tried to force a smile again. "She's good, Phil. Just tired. We're all tired. All the damn time."

"Welcome to parenthood," Phil said, grinning. "You know what they say? It'll be like this 'til you ship 'em off to college."

"I think I slept once," Gordon sighed jokingly yet honestly. "I think I slept a long time ago."

Finishing his own cup of joe, Phil screwed up the

paper cup and threw it onto the van's dashboard, where it joined a half dozen others. "Anything I can do?" He wiped coffee from his chin.

"Do?" Gordon replied, turning to his friend. "For what?"

"For you."

Gordon attempted to take another sip of coffee but quickly stifled a yawn.

"Anything to help," Phil added. "Anything I can do to make your life easier or somethin'. I dunno."

Gordon sighed. "Just do your job, Phil. Ain't nothin' else I need." He then turned his gaze away from the meadow and into his side mirror as the guard sat in a security car behind them.

This guard was speaking on a cell phone and had been for longer than Gordon was happy about.

"What's taking him so long?" Gordon mumbled to no one in particular.

The guard, meanwhile, was ending the call.

"Okay," he said, nodding. "I'll let 'em know right now."

Hanging up the call, the guard then stepped out of the car and headed toward his van. Passing on the left-hand side, he glanced at the large lettering on the doors. *Hazard Elimination Corp.*, it said in bold letters, with *Asbestos Abatement Professionals* in cursive beneath.

Rolling down the driver's side window, Gordon smiled politely as the guard peered in. "We good?" Gordon asked.

"Just spoke to Bill Griggs," the guard said in a firm tone. "Says he's getting off the ramp now. Be here soon."

"Thanks."

Phil glanced out of the passenger side window, toward the large metal sign by the gate. *No Trespassing*, it declared. *Danvers Mental Hospital. Massachusetts State Property.*

He then turned back to the guard. "Hey, let me ask you something," he said, leaning across his seat. "This place's been closed for how long now?"

"Doors shut in '85," the guard replied curiously. "Why d'you ask?"

Gordon could only sit silently as this exchange happened over him, so he turned his sights back at the meadow ahead.

"Well, I was wondering, what's with the security? Why you here?" Phil smirked. "It's not like anyone's trying to get out, right?"

"Not out, my friend. In." The guard smiled. "My job's to stop 'em from tryin'."

"Who tries to get in?" Phil asked.

"The usual sort," the guard replied, tucking his thumbs into his belt. "Kids, delinquents, bums, ex-patients." He smiled, noticing Phil's sudden look of surprise. "Oh yeah, a lot of patients ended up on the streets when they closed this place. And some come back. You'd be shocked at how many."

"No shit." Phil chuckled. "They *wanna* come back?"

The guard nodded. "Found half a dozen over the last

year alone. But they are like bats. Chase 'em off, and they, soon, come back to roost."

"Patients come *back*?" Phil replied, not able to fathom it. He could not help but laugh. "That's insane."

"It sure is somethin'," the guard added as he, too, let out a polite laugh. "Lord knows why. Wait'll you see the place, though." He grimaced before continuing. "It's so bad that I'd rather sleep on the streets." He paused and shrugged as his smile returned. "Then again, I'm not nuts."

Phil chuckled.

"Heads up," Gordon interjected, noticing a pristine, bright orange Chevy in his side mirror pulling up beside the guard's car.

Knowing his cue, the guard patted the side of the van twice and nodded to Gordon and Phil. "Good luck, fellas. You stay safe in there."

"So, what's the angle?" Phil asked.

Gordon drove the van behind the Chevy snaking up a thin winding road.

"Gotta be the cheapest, I guess." Gordon shrugged. "Environmental Solutions and Yankee Fiber were up here last week. So, I know, with us, they have three putting bids in for the job."

"Any clues *what* they bid?" Phil asked.

"I heard Yankee's were really low." Gordon shook his head dismissively. "And fast."

Phil exhaled loudly. "We will do it faster. You're gonna say that, right?" he asked, concerned. "You know Griggs. He always wants as fast as possible. We gotta beat 'em all."

"I like safe jobs, Phil," Gordon countered. "Only if they're safe. No point in doing it fast if it puts any of us in danger."

"Please don't gamble on the job one, Gordo," Phil said. "We can't afford to lose it. We will be safe. We always are. You know that. If you want, I could talk to Briggs—"

"I *know* what to do, Phil," Gordon said with a shock of annoyance in his tone. "Okay? I *know what to do*."

As he drove, Gordon peered out at something approaching. As they passed a line of trees, a colossal redbrick Victorian Gothic building came into view. Three stories high, with granite trim and sharp gable slate roofing. Its huge iron-barred windows resembled a multitude of eyes that stared outward. The concrete cornices were heavily overgrown with ivy, as was the surrounding areas. Neither the grounds nor the building itself had been tended to for many years, and it seemed that nature had attempted to reclaim this complex as its own.

"Jesus" was all Phil could say as the hospital came looming into view, his eyes widening in awe.

Chapter 2

Crossing The Threshold

As Gordon stepped out of the van, he noticed the death around him. The ivy he had seen when he drove up the path, which covered large portions of the building, was, in fact, long dead. Dried and leafless, it held onto the brickwork with a skeletal grip. It was not just the ivy either; the trees around the main building were also without any life. They were now just wooden husks that stood like monoliths.

The wooden benches that dotted around the complex were also affected by rot, looking as if they could crumble if anyone dared to sit on them.

Looking down beneath his feet at the car park's asphalt, at the long cracks that streaked through it, he pursed his lips.

"You okay?" Phil asked, sidling up to Gordon, carrying a canvas tool bag in his hand.

"This place feel like a cemetery to you?" Gordon sighed, still staring at the cracks beneath him.

Looking around at the building, Phil smiled, nodding. "Yeah." He turned, then motioned to the orange Chevy parked up a few feet away. "Dunno what Griggs wants with this place. Should be leveled if you ask me." From his tool bag, he brought out a disposable face mask and workman's gloves, then handed them to Gordon, who took them without a word.

The door to the Chevy opened, and out stepped Bill Griggs, the Danvers Town Engineer. In his fifties, he was a jolly man, with a large red birthmark splayed down one of his cheeks.

"Impressive, isn't she, gentlemen?" Bill said with pride, pointing to the building.

Phil smiled in reply. Gordon just stared, unable to muster anything.

"Eighteen seventy-one," Bill stated proudly. "That's when this Kirkbride went up."

"Kirkbride?" Phil asked.

"Dr. Thomas Kirkbride designed these kinda buildings in the eighteen hundreds," Bill explained, shaking hands with Phil and a reluctant Gordon. "This was the jewel in the crown of them." He looked again at Gordon, noticing his exhausted expression. "You not sleeping, Gordo?" He laughed.

"I'll sleep when I'm dead," Gordon replied.

"Well"—Bill turned to Phil—"he's a ray of sunshine this morning, isn't he?"

"That's why we love him," Phil replied.

"Shall we?" Gordon prompted with a sign, motioning to the building.

"It's just like a big bat," Bill said with arms outstretched, leading the way into the main foyer of the Kirkbride building. "You got your main staff building in the middle —the body, so to speak. Then, slanting off to each side, it looks like a crooked wing on the floor plan. One wing for female patients, the other for the men. Each three floors." He turned, a wide smile still on his face. "So, it may appear like a maze when you first walk around, but it's a pretty simple layout. Just remember it's a bat. Helped me to remember."

"More like a dead bat, eh, Bill?" Phil joked, glancing around the large dilapidated entrance.

"More's the pity." Bill nodded. "And you'd never know it by the state it's in, but this whole place is listed on the national historic register."

Gordon looked surprised, the first emotion other than exhaustion he had shown. "This place?" he said, looking at its rotten, peeling wallpaper, the spray-painted graffiti on the walls, the mess of leaves, papers, and dirt all over the cracked marble tiles, the broken furniture. "Why's it in such a state, then?"

"Time hasn't been kind to the old girl, and no one knew what to do with it when she closed. So, they just left her as she was. Hoping she would go away, I guess, or sort herself out." Bill shrugged to Gordon. "And because she's on the register, we can't knock her down either! And trust me, I'd love to." He sighed loudly. "The land she's on is priceless. I'd say scrap it all and build a Walmart. But, nope, it's protected being on that damn register, so we can't get rid of her." He signed, slapping his hand on the wall. "Despite only about a tenth of this place being salvageable. Has to be rebuilt and all in line with how it was back then. Historical significance or some such baloney." He looked at Phil and Gordon in turn. "So, the town manager said we gotta reclaim it starting this year, as she's got plans. So, that's what we gotta do."

"Plans?" Gordon asked.

"Gonna become the new local government building. Putting all our offices into one central location."

"Well, if it's gotta be done that way, who are we to argue?" Gordon shrugged. "A job is a job."

"Better for you guys. Headache for me!" Bill smiled again. "Let me show you some of the sights around here."

As they walked down the murky first floor hallways of the female wing of the hospital, each footstep they took echoed around them. Without any other sounds in the building, each crack of dirt under their shoes reverberated.

With Bill leading the way, he talked without turning to either Phil or Gordon. "This place, I'd love to say it had good bones, but even the bones seem to be rotten. We got one hell of a rebuild on our hands."

Coming to a halt, Phil noticed something out of the corner of his eye. Peering into an open double-door room, he saw a large porcelain bathtub placed in the middle of the space. Covered in dirt and dust, it looked strangely ominous.

Phil called out to Bill, "Hey, what was this place? Shouldn't they have a shower block? Not just one tub?"

Gordon stepped back and glanced inside. "Phil, that's hydrotherapy, not a bathroom."

"Right you are there, Gordon," Bill said, stopping, then walking back over. "This room was the hydrotherapy examination room. They'd soak the nut jobs in cold water. Cruel, really. Used to be the cutting-edge of medicine back in the day."

Phil looked at Bill, appalled. "They'd drown them?"

Gordon shook his head. "Damn barbaric if you ask me."

Bill chuckled at their reactions, and he then lay a jovial hand on Gordon's shoulder.

"'Course, if that didn't work"—Bill smiled—"they'd pump 'em up with insulin. Then put 'em in a nice coma."

"What?" Phil turned, shocked.

Bill shrugged. "That or just give 'em a full front lobotomy." His smile grew. "Suck that brain right outta them!"

Phil grimaced as Gordon scoffed.

"I'm just havin' some fun with ya," Bill quickly said. He then playfully punched Phil lightly on the arm. "Seriously, though, those lobotomies, the prefrontal ones? They were perfected here at Danvers. One of the reasons the place was as wealthy as it was. Got so much in grants for their research."

"Well, Bill," Phil said, "you're just a regular walking encyclopedia of horror, you know that?"

"Oh, this ain't me." Bill chuckled. "My wife's the local historian. She always tells me all the bits about places I'm about to manage. She likes to keep me in the know like that." His face suddenly lit up, recollecting. "Hey, you know what, guys? There's a fantastic morgue in the basement where they'd do postmortems. Some real horror stories down there you wouldn't—"

"Bill, could you just show us the problem areas?" Gordon asked. "We can have a look and tell you what we can offer, get that out of the way."

Bill's smile dropped, disappointed. He nodded, realizing that he may have come across as a bit overexcitable.

The hospital's expansive kitchens were in as bad a state as the rest of the building they had seen. What wasn't coated in dust was either dirty, broken, or covered in rat feces—or all three.

Giant aluminum pots hung from large metal frames affixed to the ceiling. Immense stoves with dozens of burners on them stretched along one wall. On the other side, large walk-in freezers, now empty, lay open without any power.

As they walked, Phil could not help but stare at the size of everything. "Damn. You could feed an army with this stuff," he exclaimed aloud.

"They did just that in the first world war. Garrisons on the way through to the ports were often allowed to use the kitchens before shipping out," Bill replied. "This place was more or less a self-contained town. Got its own church, theater, gym—hell, there was even a bowling alley."

"You could live and die here without ever leaving," Phil added.

"There's even a lovely cemetery behind the machine shop. No headstones. Just numbers. You really oughta check that out. It's something to see. Ironically, being a place of death is one of the only places with living trees and green grass."

As they exited the kitchen, they walked into a large empty room where the flooring changed from marble to vinyl tiles.

Noticing this, Gordon stopped. As the others carried on, he pulled a box knife from his pocket. With one edge of its blade, he then scraped at the vinyl tile.

Bill carried on his tour ahead. "This room'll become the Municipal archives. Was once a dining area but more recently a gym. The wife will be working here." Glancing over his shoulder, Bill soon noticed Gordon crouched behind them, who was still picking at the tile. "All okay?"

Phil stopped, too, and turned to look at Gordon curiously. "Is it bad?"

Without looking up at him, Gordon spoke to Bill. "You think there's gonna be a lot of foot traffic in here?"

"Uh, yeah, I guess so," Bill replied. "All the rooms will."

Standing, Gordon wiped the blade on his trousers and put it back in his pocket. He pointed at the tiles. "Then, all these need to go. They contain asbestos. They aren't in too bad shape and would be fine if there were minimal people here, but you should take them out to be safe."

Bill's face fell. "The other bids didn't point that out."

"Well, they should have," Gordon replied, walking up to them. "Kind of standard. The fact they didn't mention it says a lot about them as a business and what kind of expertise they actually have."

Bill nodded as his disappointment turned to a smile. "Nicely done. I'm impressed. Now, let's take you both to the female wing. Ward C. That's gotta be our main focus. It'll become the main administration building. With the bursar's office, town manager's offices, school committee, public works—"

"In other words, your office?" Gordon asked.

Bill laughed aloud, turning to lead them out of the old gym. "You got it, my friend! The most important room of all."

Walking down a third-floor connecting corridor in the female wing, Bill Griggs led the way with a confident stride, flashlight in hand. He remained waxing lyrical about all the facts of the building that he could remember, failing to notice that Phil and Gordon had lagged slightly behind.

As Gordon peered around each door, he couldn't shake the feeling of unease that had settled in his gut. Every step they had taken into the asylum felt like a step into another world, a world where hope was not part of the building's fabric.

Was it a mistake to take this job? he mused.

He glanced at Phil. They'd been through a lot together, and he knew Phil needed the job as much as he did. So, he couldn't back out. But deep down, he wanted to. Something about this place, something he couldn't place, he didn't like.

He had always considered himself a practical man, not given to flights of fancy or superstition. But here, surrounded by the decaying remnants of so many imprisoned lives, he couldn't help but feel that they were trespassing on something that didn't want to be disturbed.

"You okay, boss?" Phil asked under his breath quietly so that Bill could not hear.

Gordon smiled and nodded. "Just this place. It feels weird, right?"

"Oh, I get that. It sure is..." Phil couldn't find the right words, and he looked around. "It sure is something."

"Something indeed."

Walking through a pair of double doors, Bill strode ahead, pointing with his flashlight to a large A that adorned the wall in chipped, faded paint. He stopped, speaking in an excitable tone, clearly relishing his added job as a guide, not realizing that the others were far behind. "Each of these wings is made up of four wards, A, B, C, and D. Ward A is the farthest away from the staff building."

"Sorry, what?" Phil asked from twenty feet behind, unable to hear Bill clearly.

Turning, evidently surprised that they were not right there, Bill spoke louder. "Thought there was no time to dawdle, Gordon?"

"Apologies, Bill. Just talking about the gym tiles," Gordon said. "What were you saying about the wards?"

"Oh yeah." Bill scrambled to get back on track. "Four wards in each wing, A through D. A is here, furthest from the staff building." He pointed his flashlight to his left, down an adjoining corridor that was barred off with yellow caution tape.

This light illuminated the musty, moldy, moist brown decay. Far worse than any of the rooms they had seen before.

As Bill and Gordon looked over the tape to where the flashlight shone, a multitude of drippings could be heard. They could see that the walls, ceiling, and floors of this ward were severely water damaged. And at the far end of the corridor, light spilled in from a nearby cell and illuminated a single restraint chair left alone in the middle of the narrow hall.

"Ward A, third floor is where they kept the..." Bill paused to consider his words. "More interesting patients."

"How d'you mean interesting?" Gordon asked, unable to take his eyes off the restraint chair, which glistened with moisture and menace, no more than thirty feet away from them.

"By that, I mean psychotic," Bill clarified. "Deranged. Demented. Crazy. Lala. Gone way off the reservation. Beyond help."

"I get it," Gordon said as a chill creeped up his spine.

"So, the staff kept the most dangerous ones farthest away from them?" Phil asked, confused.

Bill chuckled, turning the flashlight away from the corridor and onto Phil's face. "Sure did. And know what they called Ward A?"

Phil shook his head, his face almost white in the reflected light.

With a smirk, Bill turned the flashlight onto his own face, creating an eerie visage. "They called it the snake pit!" He then whooped like he had just said the funniest thing on earth.

Turning the light back down the corridor of Ward A, Bill continued. "If you follow this down two more wards, it'll take you to Ward C, where we are going. But the floorboards in this ward are real water damaged. Wouldn't advise walking on 'em. Would fall straight down. We think we are just gonna hollow all this out and start again."

"How we going to get to Ward C?" Phil asked.

"Either you guys afraid of the dark?" With a smirk, Bill turned and walked over to a side stairwell.

Gordon, still mesmerized by the chair in the light coming from the far room, didn't notice Phil and Bill walking away. Even without the illumination of Bill's flashlight, Gordon found himself being drawn mentally into the ward.

He just stared. Down the corridor, down through the muck and grime. He did not know what he was looking at. He just stared, wide-eyed, as if being pulled. He could not feel the seconds passing. He didn't even blink. He did not hear either of the other men calling him from the stairwell entrance. He could only hear his own labored breathing, which matched his heartbeat. Even the sound of the water dripping down the walls drifted off into the distance and sounded like white noise. A mechanical, electric static of white noise.

Though this rotten corridor was empty, a shadow drifted across Gordon's face, as if someone was standing in front of him. Though it was not something he could see. He could only stare, feeling... something. Something was there. He was not afraid. Just enthralled. His eyelids drooped slightly.

"Hello, Gordon," a deep voice whispered, sounding as if it was far, far away yet close enough to speak softly into his ear.

Chilled, Gordon's eyes widened with a snap.

"Hey, Gordon!" Phil shouted.

Reeling, Gordon was instantly ripped away from whatever had captured his attention.

"What are you doing?"

A question Gordon could not answer.

"Let's go," Bill added.

I'm just tired, Gordon thought, forcing logic into his mind. *Just damn tired.*

Following Bill and Phil down the dark stairwell, Gordon could not shake the uneasy feeling.

As they got to the bottom of the stairs, each of them carried a flashlight.

Phil and Gordon's small lights had been clipped on their utility belts and were no match for Bill's larger one, which provided little real illumination. They just made the dirt a bit clearer.

"These tunnels connect all the buildings," Bill said, leading the way with his flashlight. "This one takes us straight to Ward C. Otherwise, we gotta go out and around, which takes too long. Faster this way." He motioned to a string of old utility lights that laced along the ceiling of the tunnel system. "These workmen's lights may be old, but I think they still work. Just need some power in them."

The stench of the tunnels hit Phil's nostrils. Making his stomach lurch.

He glanced back to Gordon, continuing behind Bill. "Don't think I've ever been in a place this moldy."

Gordon could not bring himself to speak, so he just nodded politely.

"You get used to the smell after a bit," Bill added from ahead. "But you never get used to the dark."

Gordon squeezed his eyes shut for a moment, trying to push the sense of unease away. Pushing the occurrence at Ward A to his metaphorical rearview.

The three men carried on down the tunnels. Walked single file as Gordon brought up the rear. He flashed his light around him, looking at fixtures and ducts.

Bill, still in lecture mode, said, "They used the tunnels to transfer patients, apparently. Said it was for all patients' safety."

"If the wards are wings, like you said," Phil said. "What part of the bat are the tunnels?"

"I'd call 'em the ass!" Bill chortled.

Behind them, Gordon had stopped, moved over next to one of the ducts, and pulled at its flaky white insulation. "Hey, Bill," he called out, motioning to the insulation. "All these ducts oughta be wet stripped."

Bill and Phil stopped and turned, aiming their flashlights at Gordon, who held up a peeling strip.

"When this stuff breaks up," Gordon said, "dust'll get in these tunnels, and you're basically pollinating the whole building with poison. Doesn't matter if you clean all of the wards above. You gotta do these as well, or it'll all be worth squat."

"Note it down," Bill said, already dreading the budget hit of the bid.

Emerging out of the darkness, Bill, Phil, and Gordon approached a large C painted on the wall. They then turned their path up a stairwell, which was split in half, with a tall fence running the entire way up the middle.

"What's with the fence?" Gordon asked.

"Patients one side, staff the other side," Bill said, amused. "Never can be too careful with the mad ones, I guess."

Three flights up, they arrived at another long corridor, with rooms off to each side, Ward C being almost identical to A. Same layout yet without the mold and damp. Here, it was less decrepit, and even the sunlight that managed to shine in from outside seemed somehow cleaner.

"And here we are, gentlemen," Bill exclaimed, raising his arms, motioning to all around him. "Ward C, soon to be the main hub of Danvers Town Hall." He then adopted a very well-spoken tone. "'Reclaiming the past to move into the future,' as my bosses would say."

"Hey, guys. Masks," Gordon quickly ordered, nudging Phil, pointing to the piles of white fibrous dust all over the floor.

Reaching into their pockets, both of the men pulled out their disposable face masks, then put them on.

Phil, getting another mask from his tool bag, handed it to Bill. "You probably should wear this. Not the safest thing on earth to breathe."

Bill took the mask with a polite nod and hurriedly put it on. He then noticed something new upon the wall, a crudely spray-painted red pentagram. He sighed, then pushed it out of his mind, not wanting to consider it anymore.

Gordon pointed at missing ceiling tiles. "The main danger's from them. The tiles that fell and broke caused this mess." He then slipped on a pair of gloves and picked up a chunk of tile from the floor.

"That crocidolite?" Phil asked.

"Yup. Decayed and friable, probably from the forties."

Phil, too, donned his gloves and took out his own box knife, as well as a ziplock bag. Crouching, he sliced a sample off from the floor and placed it carefully into the bag. "We'll test it to make sure."

"How bad could it be?" Bill asked. "Just replace the tiles, right?"

"No, you need to isolate this whole area, room by room," Gordon said. "Full polywrap in each, neg air machines. Also need to set up a decon room with showers—the whole shebang. This stuff will have gotten everywhere."

"It's kinda like tryin' to clean sand off a beach," Phil added.

Bill shrugged. "Well, OSHA won't let me start 'til you guys clean her up, and I gotta have construction crews in here by Labor Day." He looked Gordon squarely in the eyes. "Brass tacks. Got a guesstimate on how long you'd need here?"

Phil quickly caught Gordon's gaze and gave a stern, knowing look.

Gordon nodded, understanding his partner's message. "These rooms, the dining area, the gym, tunnels, if we really work fast but safe—'cos safety is the main factor—"

"Three weeks, Bill?" Phil interjected. "We could do it in three weeks, right, Gordo?"

Gordon, anxious, quickly cut back in. "He means two weeks. We can do it in two weeks."

Phil fell silent, surprised.

Bill smiled, nodding. "Sure. Just submit a proposal by Friday. We'll weigh your offer against all the rest. Sound okay?" He then turned and began to walk away.

Phil mouthed to Gordon, *Two weeks? Really?* He felt a mild panic creep over him.

He knew, as did Gordon, that this was a month-long job if done at normal speed. He didn't know if it could even be executed in three weeks, let alone the two that Gordon had promised.

Gordon shrugged.

"Guess you've seen enough here," Bill said over his shoulder. He then gestured to the graffiti pentagram on the wall and sighed in annoyance. "Can't wait for this place to be done up. Goddamn punks come up here constantly, tagging their crap on the walls, getting high, shooting guns, pissing everywhere—"

"Shooting guns?" Gordon asked. "What are they shooting at?"

"Let's hope at each other—"

"Whoa. What the hell's this?" Phil asked.

Turning, Bill and Gordon saw that Phil was looking into one of the small rooms that jutted out from the side of the ward, his mouth agape and eyes wide.

"You'd think that was some kind of squatters making a home, right? Decorating the walls?" Bill chuckled, walking over to the room, peering inside next to Phil. "But this is untouched from when it all closed down. This is a seclusion. Well, that's what they called the patient rooms."

Inside the very small room, a barred window let in a narrow beam of daylight. The rusted bed frame that lay against one wall was much smaller than a single, barely a size to comfortably rest an adult. On one cracked ceiling, yellow paint peeled off in tiny brittle scabs, many of which littered the concrete floor.

But what Phil was so enchanted by were the walls, hundreds of cutout images, photographs, and magazine articles plastered over every square inch. A surreal collage in this setting: an ad for Colgate, complete with a smiling, happy child staring out. A collection of political cartoons about Jimmy Carter. A small damaged print of Picasso's *Guernica* was also nestled in the middle of a set of old family photographs. Photos that were so aged that most of the images had faded to faint outlines. All that could be seen in them were the polite smiles of people probably long since dead.

"Like a glimpse inside a mad mind," Bill said, putting a hand on Phil's shoulder.

"They called it a seclusion?" Gordon said as he, too, peered at the walls inside. "Strange name for a cell."

"They were allowed to do all this?" Phil asked, walking into the room to take a closer look at all the pictures. Soon followed by Gordon.

Bill shrugged, choosing to stay, standing in the hallway and looking in. "I guess this was all part of some therapy big in the seventies. Creative expression, art therapy, and all that hokum. Supposed to help make them feel better about themselves, I guess. More at home... Ah, I'm just spitballing'. I have no idea. But sure is creepy, huh?"

Gordon and Phil both stood, scanning over the images closely.

"Kinda fascinating," Phil mused with a smile, looking over many advertisements for junk food and alcohol. "Like they were stuck in here, dreaming of the outside."

"Yeah, probably a lifer," Bill said. "Damn sad if you ask me."

Gordon squinted, glancing over a series of contrasting images. One, a happy family eating Jell-O, juxtaposed to a horrifying picture from the Holocaust, with bodies piled up outside of a crematorium in Dachau. Another, a newspaper cutout of a story about a heroic dog saving a child, next to it, a terrible image of a bloated baby swarming with flies.

"What d'you suppose was wrong with them?" Phil

asked, still scanning over images in wonder. As if looking for a hidden pattern or meaning. "This all must mean something."

"Who knows?" Bill replied somewhat curtly, barely hiding his frustration that they were still here. "Schizophrenia or just a plain garden variant nut job."

As Gordon stared at the photos, his expression was not like Phil's but the same as it was when he was staring down the Ward A corridor. When he stared helplessly at the most disturbing images on the wall, Bill's voice faded into the same faint static white noise as before. Before he could fall into this moment any more, Gordon quickly shook his head, forcing the moment away.

"Okay, that's all we need," he said, then turned back to Phil. "You done here?"

Outside the hospital, Bill led Phil and Gordon over to the van, checking his watch. "I got a little time. Wanna check out that cemetery? Seven hundred and fifty bodies buried there and—"

"Aw, goddammit!" Phil exclaimed. "Gordo, I forgot your tool bag in that seclusion place. I'll just run back in and get it, okay?"

"You know the way?" Bill asked.

Phil flashed a grin. "Middle of the bat wing, down the scary tunnels, then back up to C."

"You got it!" Bill nodded.

"Thanks, Phil," Gordon added quietly. Distracted.

With that, Phil rushed inside, leaving Gordon and Bill to stand by the van.

"Want some gum?" Bill asked, pulling out a packet to unwrap a stick, then popped it in his mouth.

Gordon shook his head with a thin appreciative smile.

"I'm not sure I ever congratulated you and Wendy on your new addition," Bill said, chewing the gum with an open mouth.

"Thank you," Gordon replied, wanting to ask something but not having the nerve. "Nice of you to say."

"Well, I'm just happy it all worked out." Bill smiled. "Me and the wife only talked about it the other day. Nothing like a child to really make it all worth it, eh?"

Before Gordon could answer, Bill continued with a laugh. "The wife sends her regards, by the way. She'd kill me if I forgot to say hi. Now, show me a picture of the tyke."

Gordon reluctantly reached into his pocket, pulled out his wallet, and slipped out a small photo of his baby from one of the leather folds.

Bill smiled, looking down at the cute photo of Emma swaddled in pink. "What you call her in the end?"

"Emmanuel Kimberly Fleming," Gordon replied with pride in his voice. "Emma for short."

"Well, isn't she just a doll?" Bill looked at Gordon, genuinely happy for him. "This little miss will change your life for the better. You can mark my words. But she will also drain your bank account like a tap." He laughed at his own joke.

Gordon smiled, then as thoughts flooded his mind with the purpose of the day, his happiness dropping. "Bill, about that. I'll... I'll match Yankee's bid buck for buck. I know they came in cheap. Peterson, a guy on their crew, let it slip."

Bill raised his eyebrow as his laugh faded. "You know that isn't the way we normally run a bidding process. You know the deadline, paperwork on my desk by—"

"We can start Monday, Bill," Gordon blurted, barely able to hide his obvious desperation. "I can be in on Monday, out the following Monday."

"A week?" Bill did not know what he was more shocked by, Gordon's obvious need for the work or the fact that his estimated timeline was suddenly cut in two. "You said two weeks? You sure that's poss—"

"I'm saying one week now," Gordon said firmly. "I got four guys ready, and I'll hire another. We can do it. Have I ever let you down? You know I'm a man of my word."

"One week. That's too fast, surely," Bill said, uncertain.

Gordon took a step closer, gripping his wallet. "I'm good for it, Bill. You know that I am. We've worked enough together to know I wouldn't bull you."

Bill stared back at him for a moment, assessing. Seeing the desperation in his eyes.

"I-I need this job, Bill." Gordon could not hide the panic in his voice. "Please, please."

Inside the seclusion room, Phil picked up the tool bag left on the floor. Having one final look around, he noticed an image of Chirco's artwork, *Mystery and Melancholy of a Street*. A painting that depicted a girl pushing a hoop down an empty street, while a long, mysterious, sinister shadow figure looms around a corner toward her.

Behind him, in the corridor, Phil was too engrossed to hear the footsteps nor had seen the shadow trace across the floor and then slink back from the doorway deep into the bowels of the building.

As evening began to settle in, Gordon sat in his van as yet another wave of exhaustion washed over him.

He knew he had to fight on and that sleep would come eventually. It would have to. After the shame of his begging, Gordon wanted to celebrate with his wife.

I'll give you this one, Bill had said. *For old time's sake. And for your kids.*

He owed Bill Griggs for that. Bill didn't have to give him the job but did so anyway. And Gordon knew that Bill could get in trouble if anyone ever looked at the bidding paperwork in detail. So, that night, despite the pain of his exhaustion, he and his wife would celebrate that lifeline.

Glancing at the passenger seat next to him, he looked at the tool bag resting on it. From out of the top, a small store-bought bouquet stuck out, wrapped in plastic, along with a bottle of cheap champagne and a box of chocolates.

Turning back, struggling to focus, he glanced over to the modest home across the street. *His* home.

He watched his wife, Wendy, potter around the front yard, watering the parched plants. Beside her, their baby, Emma, sat, crying in her stroller. As her wails got louder, Wendy quickly finished the gardening, stooped down, then picked the baby up, patting her gently on the back to calm the tears. Around them, their small dog jumped merrily, letting out little yelps of joy.

Gordon's heart ached as he watched them. This was supposed to be his sanctuary, his place of peace and comfort. But all he felt was a gnawing sense of inadequacy.

Wendy deserved so much more than this—more than a husband who was always tired, always distant, begging for the next paycheck. And Emma... She was a miracle, their little miracle. But how could he be the father she needed when he could barely keep himself together? The weight of responsibility upon him was crushing, and the fear that he might fail them both kept him awake at night. Kept him awake *every* night. He wanted to be stronger for them, to provide and protect, but every day felt like an uphill battle.

This job, though, and the possibility of a big bonus if

they finished on time, that would go some way to easing his mind.

Looking down, Gordon held pictures on his lap he kept in the driver's side door. Images of Emma's christening. He slowly leafed through them, of he and his wife. He and Phil. Emma in the arms of a priest, with his finger poised over her forehead. These photos were a—

"Gordon?"

A deep voice spoke quietly in his mind, shattering his reflective moment, causing him to glance up and around.

As his gaze fell back to his house, any concern quickly drifted away as his wife stared back at him from across the street, still holding Emma in her arms.

Gordon stared back, weary, and waved.

Smiling slightly, she mouthed the word *hello* before walking inside the house. Through the open front door, Gordon could see the kitchen, where a large pot cooked away on the stove, steam rising from boiling liquid.

Grabbing his tool bag with the presents inside, he opened the van door and stepped out.

He couldn't wait to embrace his family.

The clatter of a metal pot onto a ceramic tile.

The wailing of a child.

The frantic barking of a small dog.

And then...

...a shrill scream.

Chapter 3

Monday

T he sun had hidden behind a thick sheet of gray clouds, as if it were afraid to send any of its light down onto the old Danvers Hospital. With a humid start to the day, the overcast sky added a feeling of depressive sluggishness.

But not for Gordon and his crew. They had already been on site for a few hours, working since the moon was about to leave. Setting up generators, lighting, moving large amounts of tools to the required rooms, a mammoth undertaking.

At the front of the entrance, nestled into the weed-infested parking area, a large portable generator rhythmically grumbled along, churning out the charge from within its fuel-powered belly. Cables snaked out from its body, leading across the parking area, down the side of the building, through the aged basketball court, into the dining hall, then the kitchen and splitting off below into the tunnels.

Down there, the string of sixty-watt lightbulbs that streaked the ceilings weakly pulsed with the fed-in power, casting dull orange hues onto the grimy subterranean surfaces.

After ascending the steps from the tunnel up to Ward C, a man walked, dressed in full white hazmat overalls, and rounded the corner at the top. Over his hooded face, he wore a purifying respirator and, on his hands, wore thick yellow protective gloves.

Stepping carefully through the corridor, over cables and tools, he approached a room with a makeshift doorway made of two vertical polythene sheets.

Inside, he looked around; a vacuum unit whirred in the middle of the room, while all the walls, ceiling, and floor were covered in plastic wrap. This was the decontamination room still in the process of being constructed.

"Genny's up, and she's purring like a kitten," the man said with a muffled voice.

Gordon, wearing an identical hazmat suit without a respirator, emerged from behind one of the hanging sheets. In his hand, he held a nearly empty roll of duct tape.

He glanced at the man for a few moments, then shook his head. "Christ's sake. Take off the mask, Hank."

"We sure the ACM levels are safe?" the figure, Hank, asked.

Behind him, Phil was kneeling at the far wall beside a seclusion room. With a box knife, he cut away some overflow of sheeting.

He smirked at Hank, adding, "You get that there's no danger yet, right?"

"What?" Hank asked, turning to Phil.

His voice was barely audible through the mask.

Phil rolled his eyes. "We haven't even started gross removal." Pausing, he noticed that Hank was just staring back at him and not doing anything. "Hank, take off the mask, you dickhead!"

At twenty-nine, Hank would never consider himself a wise-ass fuck-around who's been working the same job way too long, but Phil and Gordon both would.

They knew full well he knew he didn't need the mask just yet. And neither of them wanted to play his games.

Slipping off his mask, Hank could not hide his wolfish grin.

Gordon walked past and shot him an unemotional glance. "Can you start tagging the ducts we looked at this morning?" He bent over to pick up a new roll of duct tape. "Use the green slime. We'll be wet stripping on Friday."

Hank frowned, perplexed. "Green slime?"

"What, you deaf now?" Gordon sighed, already annoyed at Hank, despite him only being in the room for a couple of minutes.

"Uh, Gordo, don't wanna tell my gramma how to

suck eggs." Hank spoke sheepishly. "Green slime means safe... Those ducts are fucking hazardous, aren't they? You meant red slime? Right? Red?"

Gordon stared back momentarily, confused.

Phil's eyes narrowed in confusion, also recognizing the mistake.

"Right. Of course," Gordon said, his temper flaring. "I said use red. So, use fucking red. No one said green. Now, get out and start spraying."

Hank nodded and, without a word, turned to walk in the other direction, toward Phil, who was taping the poly over the doorway.

"Meant to say earlier, Phil, Amy says hi," Hank said with a smarmy smile.

Phil stopped taping and glared up at him.

For a second, Hank paused and feigned an innocent look. "What? I just said Amy says hi."

He could barely contain his glee.

"Give me one fuckin' excuse, Henry." Phil grimaced. "Go ahead. I dare you. Just one."

Gordon stood, watching them bicker.

Hank raised his hands, walking away. "Don't shoot the messenger, Phil. I'm just relaying information. She told me this morning when we were in bed."

Phil tensed and gripped the roll of tape, forcing himself not to rise to the obvious bait.

Hank continued, disappearing around the corner. "She just said to say hi to you—the number two."

Angry, yet keeping as calm as possible, Phil reacted

the only way he could and flipped off Hank's general direction.

Leaving it for a few moments, Gordon then walked over to Phil. "You good?"

Phil looked up but could not answer. He just nodded and let out a grunt through his tightly bunched lips.

"Just ignore him," Gordon said. "He's a fool."

Phil nodded.

Quickly changing the subject, Gordon rubbed his eyes. "I did say green slime, didn't I?"

"Sure did," Phil replied, getting back to ripping off a new strip of tape.

"Fuck's sake. This isn't good. I'm so damn exhausted. Don't know what I'm saying." Quickly slapping his cheek, Gordon shook off any concern and turned back to his section of the room. "Just gotta focus. It's only a week we gotta do this for. *Then* I can sleep."

Mike, a lanky bespectacled man in his thirties, stood by a side door to the kitchen, loading in crates of tools and rolls of plastic. Helping by stacking the crates in the middle of the floor was the fifth and newest worker of the abatement crew, Jeff—Gordon's nephew.

At eighteen and with a mullet so severe that it would never be looked on as fashionable, he seemed content just to be there. Unlike the rest of the stone-faced crew, he had a dumb smile emblazoned on his face, not worn away by years on the job.

Mike couldn't help but chuckle at Jeff's enthusiasm. The kid reminded him of himself at that age—eager, but dammit clueless—ready to take on the world without knowing a thing about it.

As he handed the kid another crate, Mike wondered how long his optimism would last. This job, this line of work, it had a way of wearing you down. Mike had seen it happen to too many good men only after a few days.

"So, dude, how long you been working for my uncle?" Jeff asked, taking the next crate from Mike.

"Five whole, very, very long years," Mike answered. "Seems way longer, though."

"Whoa, that's a long time, dude," Jeff said, placing the crate by the others. "Hope he's not a slave driver like my dad is."

Lifting the next crate from the pile outside, Mike didn't let the conversation delay any work that had to be done. "Gordon's strict but really reasonable. Just follow the rules he has. First is, be safe. Second, do your work well. Third, do your work on time." Mike handed Jeff the next crate, looking serious. "And a big one, no drugs on the job, *dude*."

Jeff laughed, finding it all quite funny.

After walking over to his bag, he unzipped it and pulled out a boom box, then placed it on a kitchen countertop. Before Mike could say anything, Jeff slammed on the play button, and a loud barrage of squeaking guitars and pounding drums spat out of its small speakers.

"What the hell, dude?" Mike said, accidentally calling Jeff "dude" sincerely without the same mockery as before. "What's that?" He pointed to the boom box.

"That's the tunage," Jeff replied, not getting—or more to the point, not caring—that Mike clearly didn't want the music played. "So, Mikey boy, you gonna show me the ropes, then? Show me how to do all this asbestos movin' stuff?"

Stopping what he was doing, Mike gave Jeff a dry, unimpressed look. "It's just Mike, okay? Not Mikey."

Jeff smiled and nodded. "Sure thing. Mike, it is."

Passing through the room, smoking a cigarette while humming along to his own tune, Hank nodded to Mike, then stopped, noticing Jeff.

"This the new guy?" Hank asked, not taking his eyes off him.

"That there is Jeff," Mike answered.

"I'm Jeff," Jeff uselessly added.

"*You're* Jeff?" Hank smiled.

"He's Gordon's nephew," Mike added. "Play nice."

Without missing a beat, Hank pointed at the boom box. "Mike didn't tell you about that?"

Confused, Jeff looked to his boom box, then back to Hank. "Huh? What about it?"

"Can't use these on the job." Hank shrugged. "Well, not this music."

"Why not?" Jeff asked and looked to both Hank and Mike for an answer.

"Listen up," Hank said, taking a step forward.

"Music creates sonic vibrations. Bigger the music, bigger the vibrations. And those vibrations jiggle all the dust into the air. And that floating dust then gets in your lungs. So, loud music in here, bigger chance you'll breathe in the shit we're trying to get rid of." He paused for a beat. "So, aside from this, what kind of music you wanting to play, Jeff?"

"I dunno, maybe some Korn, Metallica—"

"Jaysus!" Hank exclaimed. "You wanna kill us? Look, just put it away. Or play something easy and cal... Like Yanni or some shit."

Jeff just leaned down and switched off his music with a sigh.

"Anyway," Hank said, looking at Mike, "where you unloaded the slime?"

"Red by the steps in the gym," he answered, back to loading in the crates. "Green in the van still."

"Cool. We'll see you kids at lunch," Hank said with a smile, tossing his cigarette to the cracked tiles, then stamping on it. "I'm off down. Deep, deep down, to get my slime on." Grinning, he walked away, crossing to the door leading to the gym.

Jeff stood, speechless, then turned to Mike. "Was he fuckin' with me?"

Mike just laughed.

A level under Ward C, Hank strolled happily down the length of the tunnel ahead. With his mask around his neck and headphones over his ears, he hummed loudly along to his music.

Strapped to his back, he wore a large aluminum canister, holding a hose that came off from it. With every few steps, he sprayed a viscous red liquid on any frayed areas of the duct that ran alongside him, marking it, as Gordon asked, but in the correct color.

After a few minutes, he came to a stop. Just ahead, a rusted gurney blocked his way. Jammed between the two walls. Attempting to push it to one side, Hank grunted, as it didn't budge.

"Just fucking great," he grumbled over his music. "This place is goddamn Bedlam." Awkwardly, he climbed over the obstacle and carried on his spraying.

After a long morning of prep inside Ward C as well as the tunnels that ran underneath it, the sun finally broke through the gray clouds and spilled over the hospital grounds.

The five-man abatement crew of Hazard Elimination Corp. sat on benches fixed into the dry grass across from the hospital's parking lot. The break for lunch was spent mostly in silence, as each man ate their sandwiches and recovered from the morning's exertion.

As Gordon munched on an apple, he flicked through a folder of paperwork resting on his lap.

Mike was lying on one of the benches, reading a book on true crime.

Hank leaned against a tree, enjoying the sunshine, sunglasses on, cigarette in one hand. He held a scratch card in his other and scratched off the substrate ink with a fingernail.

On the furthest bench, Phil was sitting, slowly changing a gasket from one of the respirators. Next to him, Jeff watched on, taking the lesson all in.

"You got that?" Phil asked, fitting the gasket in place. "On left, down, left 'til out clicks."

"And that's all that stops the bad stuff from getting in?"

Phil looked at Jeff with a smile, as if Jeff had told a funny joke by pretending not to know what the gasket was for. But when Phil saw Jeff's wide-eyed, honest expression, he could only nod in reply. *Poor kid*, he mused to himself. *Poor, dumb kid.*

"You know, Gordo," Hank said, crumpling up the losing scratch card, "I was thinking, you finally landed us the perfect gig. Next time someone tells us what we do is crazy, we just say, 'Yeah, well, we *do* work in a madhouse.'"

Gordon couldn't help but break a smile as the rest chuckled.

All except Phil.

"Instead of making jokes," he said without even looking at Hank, "you should be thanking Gordon. We'll all make damn good money on this one, thanks to him."

Snorting, Hank shook his head dismissively.

Looking over to Gordon, Phil smiled. "You didn't tell 'em, did you?"

"Tell us?" Jeff piped in.

Gordon tossed the core of the apple to his feet and continued reading the paperwork on his lap. "You tell 'em."

Hank turned to Phil straight on, emphasizing his attention was on the answer. "Pray tell us, Mr. Philip, sir."

Ignoring the tone, Phil smirked. "Twenty-five-thousand-dollar bonus if we finish all this on time."

Hank's face fell.

"Gordo arranged it with Bill Griggs," Phil continued. He then removed the gasket from the respirator and handed both to Jeff. "Now, you try," he said quietly.

Mike, not wanting any involvement in the conversation, carried on reading his book.

"Wait, wait, twenty-five K? What's the catch?" Hank said. "There's gotta be one, right?"

"Simple," Phil laughed. "We gotta finish by the thirteenth."

Hank slowly lowered his sunglasses as his mouth hung open. "The thirteenth? As in next Monday? A week?" His tone was incredulous, with a tinge of annoyance. He turned back to Gordon. "This is at least a two, three, maybe even a four-week job. What the hell?"

Not bothered to answer the question, Gordon just nodded, pulling out his cellphone.

With a smirk, Phil saw this moment as a cue to make

his jab at Hank. "So, I guess that means we all have to work our asses off, especially you, Hank. No coasting by on our sweat this time."

Hank did not rise to the bait. He just pushed his sunglasses back up and took a long drag of his cigarette.

Jeff fumbled, trying to place the gasket into the respirator, and it spun onto the grass below. He looked at Phil, wide-eyed and excitable at the prospect of more money. "So, we could get a big bonus?"

"I'm guessing the newbie doesn't get the same cut as us?" Hank joked, pulling out another scratch card from his pocket.

Phil could only stare up at Hank with a contemptuous look. "You want a share of it, then start pulling your weight. Simple as that. You wanna take the piss and shirk, then you can just leave, *Henry*."

The word was filled with all the disdain he could muster.

"Leave? Don't tempt me." Hank smiled, waving the scratch card in the air. "First win, and I'll definitely consider it." He turned to Phil. "Just for you. But for now, I'll just do all your work for zero credit, as always."

Gordon, lost in thought, stared at the screen of his cellphone. On it, the number for *HOME* was poised to dial.

"A scratch card?" Phil said incredulously. "That's your big plan, is it? Oh, that's really gonna take you places. Nothing like living the realistic dream."

"Don't underestimate these things. If I win, I'm outta

here! One-way ticket to Vegas! My fuckin' meal ticket!" Hank smirked to himself, knowing that his constant calm, cocky demeanor rankled Phil more than a full-out argument could do, and he enjoyed every moment of it. He paused, then pulled another cigarette out from his breast pocket and lit it.

"Hey, Jeff," Phil said, changing tack. "Mike ever tell you that smoking on the job increases your chances of getting asbestosis by nearly sixty percent?"

Jeff shook his head silently.

He may not have been the smartest of them, but he knew well enough not to get too involved in what was happening between these bickering men.

Phil turned to Hank with a smile. "You know that, Hank, right?"

Hank chuckled, inhaled his cigarette, then blew a smoke ring toward Phil.

Suddenly, Gordon snapped his cellphone shut, clearly exasperated. "Phil, Hank! Give it a rest will you, guys. It's damn tiring listening to you squawk at each other. Just make peace or just get a room and make some beautiful babies together."

Hank couldn't help but laugh. One that even made Phil smile, breaking the tension.

As this was going on, neither had noticed that the security car had pulled up or that the guard had gotten out and walked over to them.

"Howdy, fellas," the guard said loudly, startling all of the crew to turn his direction. He walked straight up to

Gordon with a handful of newly cut keys. "Got all the gate keys you wanted. One for each of ya. Just leave them on the reception desk in there when you're done."

Standing to greet him, Gordon took the keys with an appreciative nod. "Thank you kindly." He then turned and handed a key to each crew member.

As Gordon moved to each of the crew, he limped slightly.

Noticing and having seen Gordon limp earlier on, Phil opted to say nothing but couldn't help but feel concern.

The guard sat on one of the benches and exhaled loudly. "So, what d'you think of the ol' bird?"

"Bird?" Jeff asked.

The guard laughed. "The big old bird behind us," he said, aiming his thumb at the hospital. "Fifteen years really took its toll, didn't it?" He glanced around at it. "Hard to believe there used to be two and a half *thousand* patients in there. 'Specially as the place was built to house about five hundred."

"You know why they closed it?" Jeff asked.

"Was happening all over the states in the eighties." The guard shrugged. "Feds called it deinstitutionalization. So, most of the nuthouses were shut."

"This place was really over capacity by that many?" Phil asked, clearly disturbed by the prospect. "Where did they put them all?"

The guard nodded. "Single-person rooms became

space for four people. I've seen pictures that'd turn your ass hairs white with shock. They even had patients on gurneys down in those tunnels."

"So, where did they all go?" Jeff said. "When they closed it?"

"Dumped on the streets," Phil replied flippantly. "You see them crazies all over Danvers. My betting is most were from here. 'Cos they weren't on the streets when I was young."

"Either that," the guard said, "or went into other care programs if they were too dangerous or too far gone."

Looking at the key in his hand, Hank scoffed loudly. "So, the loonies are all outside in the real world, and here we are, with the keys to the looney bin. Fuckin' . Goddamn... Fucking... perfect!"

The guard chuckled. "Welcome to my life!"

"It wasn't just budget cuts or deinstitutionalization that closed this place," Mike said, lying on the bench, still reading from his book. "There was that Patricia Willard scandal in '84."

"Willard?" the guard said, thinking. "I don't recall hearing about that."

"It was big at the time," Mike continued. "Bigger than the McMartin Preschool case that came after."

"Here we go. Strap in, boys and girls." Hank grinned. "Storytime with 'True Crime Mike' is about to commence."

The guard peered at Hank curiously. "True Crime Mike?"

"Oh, don't worry. It's always good when he does this," Hank added. "The guy's a criminal encyclopedia."

Phil, meanwhile, had picked up a thick stick from the floor and, with his box knife, began whittling.

"Patricia Willard was committed by her parents here in Danvers in the mid-seventies. She was, by all counts, a manic-depressive. Well, that was the official prognosis at the time. But, really, I think it was just typical adolescent crap." He placed his book down onto the bench and sat up. "In the early eighties, this new therapy took off. Called repressed memory therapy. Shrinks were claiming that, with certain techniques, they could recover lost memories from patients."

"Yeah, I heard about that being a thing here," the guard said.

Mike didn't acknowledge him and carried on. "They said they could recover memories of traumatic events. Incest. Physical abuse... Turns out that was just the tip of the iceberg for Patricia." Mike then took a dramatic pause, looking around at the men one by one.

By then, all of the men were hanging on his every word. Even Gordon.

Mike saw his captive audience and smiled. "Patricia Willard, with the help of her shrink, recalled that, when she was ten, her father raped her. Not once. But upwards of three times a week—and over many, many years. And he didn't just rape her. He'd come into her room at night wearing a black ceremonial robe."

The guard shifted in his seat uncomfortably.

"He'd take her in a car to a wooded area," Mike said. "Not alone. Her mother and grandparents were also there. The whole family were there. Over a dozen of them. And they would take off their robes and go at it with each other. A big family orgy."

"Whoa," Jeff couldn't help but exclaim. "That's so gnarly."

"It gets way worse," Mike added. "According to her repressed memories, they'd then bring in the baby. A newborn that they had stolen that week. Mom would drive to neighboring states and steal one from a supermarket. Then poor Patricia could do nothing but watch as her mother cut out that baby's heart with what she described as a stone dagger. Then, if it couldn't get worse, Patricia was forced to drink the blood of that dead baby."

"Jesus sweet loving Christ," the guard muttered.

Hank smiled, enjoying the tale and the reactions of the crew.

Gordon's face was unlike the others, though. He just stared at Mike blankly without emotion of any kind.

"And as she drank it up," Mike continued, "the others ate the flesh. Then her father and grandfather fucked her."

"The baby?" Jeff asked innocently.

Phil, still whittling, stifled a laugh.

"Patricia," Mike corrected sternly. "Repeatedly. And this was, apparently, regular. And then, as she got older, she got pregnant often. And was forced to have abortion after abortion."

"This is dark, even for you, Mike." Hank chuckled.

"It's not over," Mike replied.

"Of course it's not," Hank countered.

"This is all public record, by the way. If you don't believe me, there are court transcripts at the library that you can all check out yourself."

"Oh, I ain't doubting you, hoss," Hank said.

"So, after each abortion, which was done at home by her father, her family then cooked the aborted fetuses on the—"

"Okay!" Phil interjected. "That's enough detail, Mike."

Jeff stared at Mike with a look of utter terror on his face.

The guard looked pale.

"Fine," Mike said with a smile. "But it was called SRAS. Which means Satanic Ritual Abuse Syndrome. It was part of all that Satanic Panic malarkey. And you were right." Mike nodded to the guard. "Danvers was a big believer in it. Some of the docs here were pioneers in the therapy. But it was more or less a modern witch hunt, as they used repressed memory therapy as fact. Because of that, a lot of families got destroyed."

"So, that memory medicine was bad?" Jeff asked, his face still showing his horror.

Mike shrugged. "Well, Patricia sued her family while she was still a patient here, backed up by the administration. And it was all set to go to trial. She wanted them all locked up and justice to be had for her and all the babies she saw them sacrifice." He paused for dramatic effect. "Then, suddenly, before it got to trial, she and Danvers dropped the suit."

"What? Why?" the guard asked.

"It's a magic bullet that destroyed it all," Mike said. "Her family dug up a physical examination she'd undergone the previous year in this place that the administration tried to bury or just ignored."

The crew were all still listening intently.

"This is gonna be good," Hank gleefully whispered to himself.

"Turns out," Mike spoke slowly, emphasizing each word, "Patricia Willard was, in fact, still a virgin."

Hank cackled.

Phil shot him a disapproving look.

Mike continued, "So, the family countersued the hospital. Accused the staff of implanting false memories into their patient's heads to keep their practices alive. And the parents won big. Almost crippling this place. It proved that the repressed memory therapy was just encouraging her imagination to create a horrific past and making her believe it was real. That case negated so much of the hospital's reputation. So, that's, as well as the budget cuts"—he gestured toward the building— "poof, all gone."

Everyone turned to the Kirkbride building, bewildered.

Gordon shook his head. "Madness, all of it."

"How do you remember something if it never even happened?" Jeff asked.

"More importantly," Hank added, "if it *did* happen, how did she forget it until that therapy? No way I'd forget seeing that."

"Well, the hospital's standpoint was that emotional trauma could force the mind to erase certain memories—"

Ignoring Mike, Hank continued. "I mean, Phil remembers every baby he's ever sacrificed. Right, Phil?"

Phil calmly held up his box knife toward Hank as a silent threat.

"Patricia Willard," the guard thought aloud. "Boy, I don't recall any of that. I've read most of the files as well. Nothing much else to do here when looking out for vandals."

"Maybe a little therapy would help you remember," Mike said with a smile.

After the laughter had died down and the guard said his goodbyes, the crew finished their food—aside from Jeff, who still ate from a large bag of potato chips—and ambled back over toward the building.

With a mouthful, Jeff turned to Mike as they walked. "How d'you know all that shit?" he asked.

"My dad was on the case," Mike replied. "And I like reading about this kinda stuff."

"Don't be so humble about your dad, Mikey boy." Hank laughed and turned to Jeff. "His dad's the goddamn state attorney general."

"Really? Wow," Jeff said, taking another mouthful before finishing the first.

All getting to the main foyer, Hank fell back to walk alongside Jeff. "You see, Mike was supposed to carry the torch, too. Be Daddy's little legal clone." He motioned to Mike, who did not look impressed. "That place you went. Tufts Law School, wasn't it?"

"Drop it, Hank," Mike warned in a monotone.

But Hank wasn't letting up.

"What was that thing you were on again, Mike, the one-year fast track?"

Eager to change the subject, Mike motioned to the bag of chips in Jeff's hand. "Another rule here, no food in any work areas."

Taken aback, Jeff was pulled from Hank's conversation and turned to Mike, annoyed. "No food? Why not?"

"He's right about that," Hank replied, silently accepting that his jabs at Mike were a bit too far, even for him. "So, listen up, mullethead. You wanna eat fiber, too? If not, lose the chips."

"Mullethead?" Jeff protested, dropping his bag of potato chips on a nearby gurney. "Least I'm not some kinda scratch-ticket loser!"

Hank laughed and patted Jeff on the back.

Gordon and Phil walked up from behind.

Phil, putting on his gloves, glanced down at Gordon's limp, then back to his face. "Tough weekend, boss?" he asked quietly.

Gordon appeared a bit perplexed by the question. That was until Phil gestured to his limp.

"Oh," Gordon replied with an embarrassed smile. "I, uh, I pulled a muscle lifting the boat trailer. Stupid, really."

"Wondered what you were up to." Phil nodded. "Mike and I called on Saturday, was gonna take you for a beer at Molly's for a bit of a celebration. You know, winning the bid an' all."

"Sorry about that," Gordon replied. "Was just a bit hectic."

"Emma still got the ear thing?" Phil said.

Gordon nodded. "It'll get better." His words then trailed to a whisper. "At least I hope it does."

"Hey, listen," Phil said in a hushed tone out of earshot of the others. He then stopped to face Gordon as the others walked farther into the building.

"What is it?" Gordon asked.

"We're all psyched we got this gig, and all of us are damn grateful," Phil said, his voice still low. "But, Gordo, we gotta talk about it. If we can't make the Monday deadline—"

"Bill Griggs likes jobs fast. Remember?" Gordon replied defensively, not watching the volume of his voice as Phil did. "What else was I to do? Let another company snag this from us? For what? The sake of a few days' hard graft?"

Phil smiled, though he had no confidence in any of the plan. "I know that, but look at the men we got here to help. If we lose that bonus—"

"We won't. Look, I know what you're trying to say. Jeff'll work out. He's just a little green, that's all. You just need to push him a bit."

Phil shook his head. "It's not Jeff I'm talking about, and you damn well know it."

Gordon sighed.

He's heard this from Phil many times before.

Phil continued. "We ran into Craig McManus at Molly's. Told him about the job. About the bonus."

"You told him? Why the hell d'ya do that?"

"Gordon." Phil's smile stayed, but his tone grew more serious. "Craig said he'd quit Yankee and work for us. Besides, he's way more experienced than Hank. And he gives a shit about doing the job right, which Hank doesn't. I have to redo most of what he does anyway."

Shaking his head, Gordon took the gloves from out of his back pocket and started putting them on. "Phil, what's your job here?"

"I'm—I'm your crew super."

"Right." Gordon looked at him seriously. "You keep things moving. Eliminate obstacles, keep the crew on track. That's your job."

"I know that."

"Listen, if I thought Hank was a liability, yes, I'd be

the first to let you cut him from the crew. Okay? But he's not as bad as you're making out."

Gordon's tone stopped the conversation in its tracks.

Phil nodded but did not hide his annoyance.

"Now, let's go finish that decon chamber," Gordon said, limping back toward the kitchen.

For a moment, Phil glanced at Gordon walking away and wished he could punch some sense into the man.

With all of them back, some of the crew worked harder than others.

Hank, with his mask on, headphones on, hummed down the tunnels, spraying more red slime onto the ducts. He only did enough to get by, never any more. Walking by graffiti that simply said *Satan Rules*, he stopped for a moment and sprayed it jokingly with slime.

In the kitchen, the boom box was tuned to an easy listening radio station that played slow, low, inoffensive background muzak. Something that rankled Jeff, but he was too busy trying to complain, and Mike was too busy trying to teach him how to use the electric tile puller, a large device much like a driven lawn mower.

With both men wearing their masks, the mini-zamboni-like machine sputtered as it remained in neutral.

Mike thought teaching Jeff how to drive it would be

more fun than the rest of the work they had to do. And could be something the kid would be good at. But Jeff sat on the machine, distracted, barely even looking down at the levers and buttons.

"You know," Jeff said in full flow, looking at Mike, the tile puller chugging away without moving. "I got a second cousin who's a lawyer."

Mike waved dismissively. "Please, shut up and just pull the damn handle on the panel. Let's get you driving this thing," he said, quickly reaching the end of his tether with Jeff's nonstop questioning.

Jeff peered down and, instead of pulling the lever, looked confused at the control panel and pressed a button. Suddenly, the machine lurched forward as it hit a kitchen countertop.

"Jesus." Mike reached over and took the tile puller out of drive. "Are you a goddamn lobotomy case or something?"

"Hey, fuck you, man."

Before anything more could be said, the tile puller suddenly lost all power, and at the same time, the boom box's music cut out.

"Now what the hell did you do?" Mike exclaimed.

"I didn't do shit. I ain't touched a thing!"

Mike shook his head, waving over to the plug box. Following the cable leading away from the tile puller, he saw that nothing had been disconnected.

Exhaling loudly in frustration, he looked down at the orange cable that trailed into the gym, down the stairwell, and into the tunnels. "You better go down there, Jeff, and check the breaker box. Fuse probably blew out."

Jeff's demeanor quickly changed from defensiveness to nervousness. "Oh man, I can't go down there. No way."

Pausing for a beat, Mike slowly turned, expressionless and unimpressed. "Okay... and why is that, Jeff?"

"I got nyctophobia."

Mike stared, astonished that such a big word would come from someone like Jeff. Someone he considered having a severely limited vocabulary who was restricted to two-syllable words.

"Nyctophobia? Really?"

"It's a fear of the dark, man."

"Yeah, I got that," Mike replied, pulling his mask down, then headed off toward the gym. "Look at the manual on the counter. Study it before I get back... Mullethead."

Jeff let out an annoyed sigh.

He had come to the realization that if he stayed working for his uncle any longer than this one job, then "Mullethead" would become his nickname for sure—whether he liked it or not.

Following the orange cable across the gym, Mike walked

down the steps split by the high fence and into the tunnels below.

As soon as his feet left the stone step and hit the dirt-covered floor, Mike felt a wave of coldness. With the utility lights across the ceiling being quite ineffective, he fumbled for the flashlight hanging from his belt and switched it on without much sense of urgency. Unlike Jeff, Mike didn't mind the dark. In fact, he found it mostly calming.

Stepping through a low doorway from off the side of the tunnel, Mike followed the orange cable along the floor to an industrial-sized breaker box. One that brimmed with many cables. Next to it, the orange cable lay unplugged and on the dirt.

"What the hell?" Mike moaned before immediately guessing who the culprit most likely was. "Fuck you, Hank. You're not funny. Not funny at all." Stooping, he grabbed the plug and jammed it back into the breaker.

Out of earshot from where he was, the easy listening from the boom box started up, and Jeff whooped loudly.

Before leaving the tunnels, Mike's flashlight caught a glimpse of a second plug lying on the dirty floor. Following that cable, he noticed it trailing into a partially opened doorway at the side of the room. His light beam snagged the sign on that door that read *Staff Library*.

After plugging this second cable in, a bright light suddenly blinked on from within the far room.

Unable to quell his curiosity, Mike walked over, then pushed the library door fully open. A utility light hung off of a small broken chandelier inside. A beam that revealed many rotten shelves around the room, each packed with moldy books and boxes—the smell of which hit Mike's nostrils hard.

Wrinkling his nose, he persisted.

Turning the flashlight off, Mike walked into the library and perused the surrounding shelves. The lower ones next to him were full of boxes containing out-of-date technologies: dictation machines, reel-to-reel tape recorders, mimeograph machines.

As he looked around, the utility light suddenly flickered and lost strength for a few moments, casting the room into a temporary dark-brown hue.

As it did, Mike grabbed his flashlight, ready to turn it on, but the power resumed as quickly as it had disappeared, illuminating the darkness of the space again.

Resuming his snooping, Mike scanned more shelves. On one, piles of yellowed handwritten documentation lay loose on the shelf, each held down only by paperweights. He glanced over these pages and could tell they were all reports regarding finance.

Boring, he thought.

On the shelf below, he then noticed a box labeled *Diaries.* With a more interested shrug, he pulled the box out a little bit, reached in, and took out a small leather-bound book from the top of the pile.

Opening the book up carefully, its pages were brittle

with age. He turned to a random page in the middle and began to read.

August 7, 1975

It's been three months since I got here. Every day's just the same—same routines, same treatments. The docs have me doing this hydrotherapy thing. It's supposed to calm me down, but I just feel cold. So freaking cold. The water gets into my bones, and sometimes it feels like they're trying to drown me.

Today, while I was there, I overheard the nurses talking about a new girl in Ward A. They said she screams all night and won't stop. I wonder if she knows that no one hears her here? No one ever hears us. Not here. The walls are too thick, and the doctors don't care.

There's this one nice nurse, though. Her name is Evelyn. She sneaks me extra blankets when she can and sometimes even a piece of chocolate. I don't know what I'd do without her little acts of kindness. She reminds me of my aunt, the way she used to take care of me before the accident.

I keep praying that one day they'll let me out, that they'll realize I don't belong here. But every day, that prayer seems more unlikely. The other patients, they've been here so long, they've forgotten what the outside world looks like. I'm scared I might end up like them.

My hope is people remember who I was and not just a number on a ward.

I don't want to be forgotten.

Mike paused, closing the page gently and turning to the inside front cover. There was no name written, just two scrawled words that said *My journal*.

He felt a pang of guilt. Without a name on this book, the person who wrote it had probably been forgotten after all.

That was too deep for him to read any more, so he placed the book back in the box and moved onto the next set of shelves.

He walked over and scanned one that carried a selection of small boxes crammed into the shelves tightly. Each of them were sealed with a bright yellow tape that almost glowed in the light. Across the front of every one, a sticker boldly exclaimed EVIDENCE.

"Now, *that's* more like it," he uttered, unable to control a smile climbing his face. His interest more than piqued, Mike hurried over to the shelf and grabbed one of the boxes at random. Tugging at one's edge, he heard a loud crack sound from the frame of the shelf. Moving that box, even a tiny amount as Mike had, had disrupted the delicate balance of wooden decay and weight distribution. So much so that the whole unit almost immediately split down the middle and leered forward.

Mike managed to leap backward and out of the way of the cascading boxes that hit the solid floor with an almighty crash.

Pushed by his own curiosity, Mike didn't even stop to see if anything else could fall around him. Instead, he grabbed one box that lay nearest to him, then carried it over to the table in the middle of the room. Not even attempting to clear up the mess of the others.

Studying the box, he noticed the yellow tape was actually security tape—and not tape he could remove with his fingernails. Mike grabbed a small Swiss Army knife from his pocket and, with a smile, opened the blade and placed it under one edge of the seal—

Further down the tunnel, Hank suddenly clawed at his left eye, as a piece of dust got caught under his eyelid, scraping his cornea.

Up in Ward C, Gordon yelped, dropping his box knife to the floor with a clatter, having sliced his thumb open while cutting through some poly sheeting.

"Shit," he exclaimed through gritted teeth, staring at the beads of blood crawling out of the new cut dropping to the floor beneath him with a splat.

Unaware of any synchronicity, Mike finished cutting around the circumference of the box's security tape, then lifted off the lid. Peering down, his expression showed a mixture of curiosity and confusion.

Above him, the lightbulb crackled and dimmed ominously. He reached inside to pull out the contents.

With the sun beginning to set on the crew's first day at the Danvers State Hospital, Gordon sat on the edge of the back of his van, putting a Band-Aid on his thumb. He was dirty, sweaty, and utterly exhausted, even more than the day before.

On the bench a few feet away, Hank was stripping off his hazmat suit with a grimace. His very sore-looking left eye was bloodshot.

Jeff was next to Gordon in the van, staring at the building in a daze. He never expected the work to be as intense as it had been. At that moment, he wished he was brave enough to tell his uncle that he didn't want to come back the next day.

Phil walked over, wiping the sweat from his neck, and looked down at Gordon, who was finishing off his first aid.

"You slice an artery, boss?" he asked.

"Just a nick," Gordon replied. "Nothing to report."

Phil smiled weakly. His tiredness evident. "It was a good first day, Gordo. A really good one."

Without even looking up, Gordon replied gruffly, "I know that. Don't tell me, Phil. Tell *them*. They are your responsibility."

Frowning, Phil then changed the subject. "Mike said he's gonna stay another hour or so. The genny's been acting up. Carburetor needs cleaning, he thinks. He doesn't wanna hold the work up, so will do it now. He's just in the gym waiting. Won't be a sec."

"Okay," Gordon replied, then looked up at Phil

sternly. "But I don't want anyone hanging out here when it's dark. Understood? Tell him that."

Phil nodded. "I'll tell him." He turned to look at Jeff, then at Hank. "Good job today, you guys."

Hank rolled his eyes. "Oh yeah. Right. If it keeps up like this, we'll all be fuckin' dead by next Monday." He threw his hazmat suit in a pile on the grass beside him, then reached for his boots to put them back on.

As he walked by, Phil clipped Hank on the side of the head with his hand. "Pick up your shit, Henry," he mocked, strolling away toward the building.

Hank, for a second, lost any cool demeanor. "And fuck you, too, Phil!"

Phil smiled without turning back.

He felt like he had won that small battle.

Chapter 4

The First Session

Hissing static from a quarter-inch reel-to-reel crackled throughout the tunnels.

As Mike sat in the dank staff library, he watched the reel spin.

Having wiped mold off from the player's tape heads, then wired a new plug to the machine, he was shocked that it had fired up perfectly. Just as it would have done when it was first bought. For a few moments before plugging it in, Mike dreaded the worst, that the speakers could have been broken, but as the static sounded, he punched the air victoriously.

Though after a few minutes of listening intently, watching the reels spin and exchange its tape from one to the other, Mike sighed. "Just my damn luck," he mumbled, picking up the tape's cardboard box. He looked at the typed label on the front.

SESSION 1
MARY HOBBES
age: 34
(*ALTERS: The Princess, Billy, Simon*)

Dropping the box onto the table, he resigned himself to the fact that he was probably wasting his time.

Leaning over, he flicked the fast-forward switch as a last attempt, which sent a wash of a higher-pitched hiss out of the speaker.

After a few moments of the same scratching static, just as Mike was about to give up and get back to work, a sudden squealing jumble of noises sounded.

He immediately released the switch and hit play.

"April 3, 1984," a deep-voiced man sounded over the reel-to-reel speaker. *"Patient is Mary Hobbes, female, age thirty-four. This is session one of her recorded annual evaluation. The patient is in restraints due to an earlier violent incident."*

————

Doctor David Adams stared at the open file on the small metal table in front of him. Peering over his thin glasses, he scanned his handwritten notes. His thin face, long goatee, and intent stare earned him the secret moniker of Ming the Merciless among the patients of the hospital—not that any of them would ever dare mention that name to his face, as they feared him.

As a respected psychotherapist among his peers, he was seen as a man who would not stop until he got what he wanted from a patient, no matter the cost. Normally, at the cost to the patient's health.

Across from him, Mary Hobbes sat in a restraint chair, dressed in a tatty patient's gown. She sheepishly looked to the floor. Her hands and feet were strapped down tight, her head shaved poorly, with clumps of hair dotting her skull. A standard look among the other shorn patients.

"I'm sorry about before," she mumbled, catching the doctor's attention. "I don't remember doing any of that, but I must have done it. Right?"

"Right," he said. "But that was then. Now, with whom am I speaking to this morning? I presume Mary?"

"Yes, it's me." She smiled weakly, peering at him. Her voice was raspy and sore from hours of crying and screaming in her room, as was the norm for her.

"And how do you feel this morning, Mary? Are you well?"

Mary shrugged as best as she could in the restraints. "Okay, I guess."

"Good." The doctor picked up a pen from the table and flicked through her file until he landed on a blank page. "And how have things been going for you in general this year? How has your treatment progressed?"

"I don't know. Good?"

A tremble in her voice belied her words.

The doctor began to scribble notes on the page. "I'm

glad to hear that. And with that in mind, maybe this is the year that you want to talk about why you did what you did twenty-four years ago? We have given you enough space of being able to avoid such a subject."

"I told you I didn't do anything."

"Are you saying that you still don't remember what occurred?"

"No. I never said that. I remember everything. But like I said, I didn't *do* anything."

"I know this is very difficult, Mary. That's why we're here to help. After all this time, you have to know that, don't you? Now, tell me, are you not saying that because it's just too painful for you to talk about, or do you just not care anymore about what you did? The deaths you caused?"

The doctor noticed Mary's leg shaking up and down, her body trembling.

She quietly began to sob. "It's been so long... I miss Danny. I miss him so much."

The doctor began to write on the pad in block capitals:

SUBJECT IS SHOWING AGITATION.
BODY TREMBLING...
POSSIBLE ALTER EMERGING?
PURSUING.

"Mary, listen," the doctor said, putting down his pen, then looking directly at her as she trembled. "I want you to remember what happened. On Christmas day. In Lowell."

"Th-That's where we all grew up," Mary said, her voice barely audible.

"Tell me what happened that day."

"N-N-Nothing h-h-appened," she said, as if her voice was closing the words off to her.

"Mary, tell me."

"N-N-Nothing."

Her next words were strangled.

"Tell. Me."

His voice turned stern.

Her eyes widened in a panic as she trembled more and more.

The doctor persisted. "Something *did* happen. That's why you're here. Why we are *both* here now. It's time, Mary. It's time. In fact, it's long overdue. You *have* to tell me. You have to."

Mary's body suddenly stopped trembling as if the power was cut to it. Her head lolled as she slumped in the restraint chair, breathing shallowly.

"Mary? Are you okay?" the doctor asked, his tone flat and disinterested. Only saying those words to elicit a response, not through genuine care.

A chuckle in a high-pitched voice escaped from her mouth. "I like Christmas," she said in a childlike, innocent tone.

A far departure from her previous raspiness.

———

"What the hell?" Mike gasped, staring wide-eyed at the reel-to-reel. "That's ... Wow."

The session's audio continued playing as he looked at the cardboard tape box again.

"*Who am I speaking with?*" the doctor asked. "*Is this Princess?*"

Mary began to reply, but it was too quiet on the tape for Mike to hear her words.

Leaning forward, he turned up the volume on the machine.

"*I'm looking for my dolly, but I don't know where it's gone. Do you have it, mister?*"

Her voice was almost too loud as it played through the speaker in a piercing treble.

"*No, Princess. I haven't. Maybe Billy knows where your dolly is.*"

Confused, Mike read the tape box again. *ALTERS: The Princess, Billy, Simon.*

"*Oh, Billy is so silly,*" Princess giggled. "*Hey, look at me, I'm a poet, and I don't half know it!*"

"This is crazy," Mike mumbled, chuckling at his ironic choice of words.

"*Princess. Can you tell me what happened on Christmas twenty-four years ago, at your house in Lowell? What you did back then?*"

The recording played, with the loud voices from the

past filling the air and echoing down the tunnels under Ward C.

"I remember that we all played in Danny's room. It was fun."

The sound drifted up the stairs and into the third floor of the ward.

"Mary got a dolly, and Danny got a big ol' knife because he's a real big boy."

"Who played in his room with you?"

The doctor's voice could be faintly heard.

Behind a sheet of opaque plastic in the decontamination room that Gordon and Phil constructed, the setting sun beamed its final warming rays through the half-boarded-up window, revealing someone standing behind it.

Listening.

Motionless.

"Mary, Danny, and me and Billy, silly … Look, I rhymed again!"

In his house, having arrived home an hour before, Hank was sitting in his lounge, miserably silent and cradling a beer.

His girlfriend Amy stood in the doorway to the kitchen with a look of hate as she shouted at him in fury. Pointing at him to emphasize every word of insult she screamed.

When she finished, Hank didn't reply, and she slammed the door shut as she left in a blazing rage.

"Has Billy told you what happened that day?" the doctor asked.

Jeff stood in his shower, scrubbing his skin thoroughly for the third time, feeling like the white asbestos dust was inside of him. He had already brushed his teeth twice, swearing he could taste the hospital still.

As he prepared for an early night, he hated the fact that he had to go back. Not just for himself or the money he wanted but to not let down his uncle or anger his father.

"Billy only tells me nice things. Like that I'm pretty," Princess replied with a giggle.

In Molly's Bar, the night had sent many drinkers home for dinner. All except Phil, who sat quietly at the bar, brooding.

He stared at his reflection in the mirror across the bar. Hating how miserable his life had become. Hating how Amy had left him for someone else—Hank of all people.

He took a swig of his drink and slammed another five-dollar bill on the counter.

"Hit me," he called out to the bartender.

"Princess? ... Was Simon there that day, playing with Danny?" the doctor asked with trepidation. *"Did he play with Danny?"*

Mike suddenly looked alert, piqued by the mention of Simon.

"Simon? I don't know anyone called that?" Princess replied. *"Now, do you know where my dolly is? I miss her."*

As the moon came out fully, a heavy rain began to fall on the town of Danvers, and Gordon sat in his van in silence.

Parked across from his house, he stared at the window wipers as they thumped left and right, clearing rain off the windshield in a loud rhythm over and over.

Looking down at his left thigh, he slowly prodded at it with his finger. Instantly, a shock of terrible pain shot through him, making him wince and let out an agonized moan.

Grunting in anger, he shook his head violently, trying to push away the pain.

Attempting to regain his composure, he glanced out of the driver's side window, toward his house.

But saw no wave of welcome this time.

No wife. No baby. No dog.

The house was dark, and all the shades had been drawn.

He wondered if Wendy would ever forgive him and come home.

"Billy's never told you about Simon, has he?" the doctor persisted.

"No... I'm tired, mister doctor." Princess was starting to sound weak. *"Let me sleep. Let us all sleep."*

"Maybe Billy would like to talk?"

"Billy's asleep, mister doctor. He's asleep. Everyone's asleep."

Mike looked in the evidence box, down at the other reels. All were marked as *Sessions*. All numbered up to Session number 9.

Chapter 5

Tuesday

As the sun rose over the Danvers horizon like a slumbering giant, its beams of pale orange light glistening upon the drops of morning dew and sparkling on the tall wild grass around the edges of the hospital. From high up in one of the top windows of the large Kirkbride building, something peered down at the crew arriving in their cars for their day's labor. Watching their every move.

"And good morning to you all, abatement professionals," Phil called out, his arms outstretched in welcome. Standing in his hazmat suit on the porch overlooking the parking lot, he grinned widely. "Let's get our asses in gear. It's time to make the donuts!"

Hank grabbed his work gear from the trunk of his battered Chrysler and then, with one hand on his car, kicked off his boots, ready to suit up. He looked as if he hadn't slept at all.

Phil noticed this and felt a warm glow of satisfaction. "What's wrong, Henry ol' pal?" he chirped happily. "On another bender last night? Huh? Getting too old to drink that much?"

Without missing a beat, Hank zipped up his overalls, then stared, stone-faced, at Phil. "Nah, man. It's just Amy. You know how she likes to experiment in the sack? She wouldn't let me sleep. Had to go again and again and—"

"It's way too early for this, guys," Mike said, getting out of his own car, looking just as tired as Hank. "Can we wait 'til after lunch to kill each other?"

His hazmat suit was slung over his shoulder.

"For you, Mike, sure thing." Phil chuckled as Hank shook his head dismissively.

"Where's Gordon?" Jeff asked, getting out of Mike's passenger seat, already geared up and ready to work, having dressed at home.

"Gordo's been here since seven, an hour earlier than I was," Phil replied. "You know, he's working his ass off for your bonuses. So, everyone better bring their A game to the whole job. Get it? Not one of us can slouch."

"What? I'm here. I'm ready to work!" Jeff protested. "We were told to get here at nine, not seven!"

From the top window, a figure slinked back into the darkness across the dusty, bare floorboard. It made no sound as it stepped over items that had been neatly laid out from one side of the room to the other, a flattened-out, finished packet of potato chips, several boxes of respirator gaskets lined up in a row, used dust masks displayed in an orderly fashion. The figure crossed the objects, careful not to disturb the display.

Jeff wished to himself that the day would end quickly. Even though they had only been working for an hour, it felt like an eternity.

Think of the bonus, Jeff, he repeated in his mind as a mantra to get him through the hours. *You'll be able to get that guitar, maybe even a car.* These thoughts pushed him forward.

Holding up a heavy canister, he poured fuel into the powerless outdoor genny. As the liquid rushed in, Jeff closed his eyes for a second, gaining some needed mental peace. He listened to nothing but the liquid flowing and the birds in the far trees, blocking out all other sounds.

But soon, the genny was filled, and after he pulled its starter cord, all the noise resumed. The clattering of the generator roared to life. The peaceful sounds drowned out.

With polyethylene sheets covering all its walls and floors, a makeshift containment room was complete on what was a seclusion in Ward C.

An opaque, hermetically sealed chamber, every edge was closed and every surface covered. In one corner, an air vacuum hummed quietly, creating negative air pressure inside, its job to allow no asbestos fibers out.

The only part of the room not enclosed was the ceiling. The ceiling with the asbestos tiles that needed to be removed.

On a ladder in the middle of the room, Phil stood on the highest step, fully suited and masked, reaching up high for a tile. Carefully pulling one out, he turned to wait for a waste bag to be brought to him.

Over by a window, Gordon was slowly stacking full bags marked with hazardous waste warnings across them. Packing the last one, something caught his attention outside the window, through the plastic sheeting.

On the ground beyond the parking lot, he noticed a crumbling set of wooden stairs that descended from ground level into woodland opposite. He found himself staring intently without cause. Just zoning out for a moment.

"Gordon?" Phil called out.

Gordon couldn't hear. He just stared out, unresponsive. Unsure of what he was really staring at. He was captivated by the dilapidated steps.

Phil looked over, annoyed. "Hey, Gordon!"

Snapping out of it, Gordon's attention was grabbed, and the spell broke. He turned, blinking, took a deep breath, and got his head back in the game.

"C'mon, let's move. I need to bag this bitch," Phil said, waving the asbestos tile at him.

Nodding, Gordon grabbed a new waste bag from a box on the floor, then opened it, walking over to Phil.

Beneath the mask, Gordon couldn't see his partner's look of concern.

"She's all topped off and purring like a kitten," Jeff exclaimed, entering the kitchen, his mask slung around his neck.

He was physically ready but mentally dreading getting back to the manual labor ahead of him.

Mike, fully suited with his mask, was ripping up a floor tile. "Good. Make sure she stays that way." He threw the tile onto the small pile of others in front of him. "Don't want her dying on us, so best check every other hour, okay?" Mike glanced up at Jeff and shook his head. "And put on your mask, princess. Don't wanna be coughing up blood, do ya?"

Jeff smirked, unimpressed, pulling up his mask to put it on. "I'm not your princess."

"What?" Mike stopped for a moment and looked over to him, with no idea what he meant.

Jeff, though, was already distracted by other thoughts in his head.

"Meant to say earlier, what's up with Phil and Hank? They're acting like my folks. Always snapping at each other for no reason. Aren't they friends?"

"I thought it was obvious," Mike replied, placing a

piece tile in a waste bag. "Hank went and stole Phil's girlfriend, Amy."

"Amy?"

"Yeah." Mike laughed. "It's our own little soap opera. They *used* to be really good friends. Then that happened." He paused for a beat. "But, Jeff, if I were you, I wouldn't get involved in any of it or mention it to them. You don't want Phil on your bad side. If you are, he'll give you all the grunt work, and it'll never end. Also you don't want Hank on your bad side either, or your life will be all practical jokes and bitchy comments. So my advice is play nice with both of them for an easy time here, you get me?"

Hank strutted down the tunnels, carelessly spraying the exposed ducts with more red slime, marking them for removal. With his headphones on, he moved each step to the beat in his head. The string of utility light bulbs along the tunnel pulsed with a dark-orange and brown glow.

Passing an open doorway that led into a pitch-black room, he stopped.

Peering in, he continued to hum. But that soon stopped as a glimmer caught his eye from the floor at his feet.

Glancing down, he saw a small metallic disc reflecting the dull light of the tunnel. Slowly, he crouched and picked it out of the dirt.

Hank's eyes widened, realizing that what he found was a coin.

Rubbing the dirt from it on his sleeve, he took another look, holding it up to the nearest light. On one side was an image of Mercury sitting on a throne. Beneath that, a date, 1866.

"Jesus." Hank smiled. "Eighteen motherfucking sixty-six! Wow."

Removing his headphones, he pulled out a small flashlight. Switching it on, he scanned the floor for more of these coins. He could see nothing in the immediate vicinity, but the beam quickly caught another glint half sticking out of a low small crack down in the crumbling wall.

After slowly walking over, he grabbed hold of the edge of the coin, then pulled it out. He laughed victoriously, realizing that this coin was a few years older than the first.

Getting on his knees, he took a closer look at the crack. Shining his light into it, he hoped to see something, anything, but it was too dark inside—yet he could tell that this was a hole, not a small crack. There was space behind it. Somewhere the coin had come from.

Smacking the crack with the butt end of his flashlight, he had expected to hear a stone thud of brick, but what came out sounded hollow.

"You gotta be shittin' me," he said, still laughing. He banged the brick harder, as a faint clinking could be heard from within.

"Jackpot," he said. "This is too good." With another swift, heavy hit from his flashlight, the brickwork soon cracked further. As chunks of stone dropped, he hacked away again and again, and the crack opened even wider. Through it, another coin tinked out and fell to Hank's feet.

Without even stopping to pick it up, he smashed the rest of the crack harder and harder until it opened wide enough for him to jam his fingers into it. When he could, he thrust them in blindly, grabbed a side of the wall, and pulled a big chunk of rock away, exposing the hole beyond. And as he did, more coins tumbled out.

Almost hyperventilating with excitement, Hank peered to his left and right, checking that he was still alone. When he had managed to convince himself that it was all clear, he smashed the edges of the hole more and more with his flashlight. Even *more* coins fell out.

"Fuck me," Hank exclaimed, thrusting his hand into the gaping stone hole.

Pulling out a fistful of coins started a torrent of others to follow from within. Dozens upon dozens of silver discs poured onto the dirty tunnel floor: one-dollar Indian heads, quarter eagles, silver dollars.

Hank stared, wide-eyed, cupping a handful from off of the floor. He loosened his grip, watching the coins slip between his fingers one by one. His Cheshire cat smile became wider with glee.

Quickly, he shoved the coins into his pockets. But

there were simply too many to carry. What he had in front of him was almost an embarrassment of riches.

He whipped his head about, glancing around for a container, for anything to stash this find, when—

"*Lunchtime!*" Phil exclaimed over the walkie-talkie that hung from Hank's belt.

The sudden audible intrusion caused Hank to jolt, and he put his hands behind his back, trying to hide the treasure. But, of course, no one was there.

"Fuck," he said in relief, realizing that he was not being watched and the voice was on his walkie.

"We'll eat at the gazebo today, guys, on the east side opposite the gym." Phil took a brief pause, then continued. "Yo, Henry, come back."

Hank was motionless, like a deer caught in the headlights.

"Hank," Phil repeated, "come back. Pick up, pick up, pick up."

Shaking his head, Hank dropped the remaining coins onto the pile below, then grabbed his walkie. Clicking the talk button, he could not mask his annoyed tone. "Yeah. What's up, Philip?" He almost snarled.

"I want you with Jeff and Mike after lunch in the kitchen. So, bring your gear up with you. Got that?"

Hank peered down at the enormous pile of coins, then back to the hole in the wall. A hole he thought could contain even more riches. He clicked the walkie button again. "Alright. Out." He clipped the device onto his belt.

With only a moment to consider the circumstances and to make any sort of plan, he quickly grabbed the coins and stuffed them back into the hole.

Little did Hank know, beyond the wall he had smashed open, inside the darkened room he had recently stopped in front of, a metal table rested in the middle of the room. Along the nearest wall, on the other side, where Hank peered into, were a series of large metal drawers. On the dirt floor next to them, fallen from the half-open door masked by darkness, a small sign lay unseen. It had upon it a single word stenciled *Morgue*.

At the rickety wooden gazebo situated on the eastern side of the hospital grounds, Phil walked over with a selection tray of Chinese takeout boxes balanced on one hand and a wallet in the other, the latter which he tossed to Gordon.

"Receipt in there?" Gordon asked, catching it.

"Uh-huh." Phil nodded before turning around to the rest of the crew, who all sat on benches facing each other. "Okay, boys, let's all thank Uncle Gordon for lunch, shall we?"

Jeff looked up from reading a yellowing piece of paper and smiled. "Thanks, Uncle Gordon."

"Your turn to buy tomorrow, Hank," Phil said, quickly handing out the boxes of noodles, along with pairs of chopsticks, to each person.

Hank, lying on a bench with his sunglasses on, chose

not to reply. He kept quiet, thinking of the coins, what they could be worth, how he could escape this place.

Phil quickly realized that one member was missing from the crew's lunch. "Where's Mike at?"

"He wanted to see if he could find the lost respirator gaskets," Jeff replied.

Gordon glanced at Jeff, then at Phil, with a look of irritation. "What did I say, Phil! I don't want anyone just wandering off by themselves. Jesus."

Not replying to this, Phil stood over Hank, reached into the food tray, and pulled out a couple of scratch cards. Dangling them over him, Phil smiled. "Don't say I never do anything for ya, Henry."

"Just give 'em over." Hank sighed. "I gave you the cash, so not like you bought me anything."

"Sure, and you're most welcome."

Smirking, Hank sat up and took the cards from him. Looking at which ones were bought, his expression dropped. "What is this? Number 2s?" He sighed loudly. "I asked for Blackjack."

"I *said* you're welcome." Phil smiled, walking away to another bench to sit down.

Down in the staff library room, Mike was sitting at the table, having neatly arranged the session tape boxes in front of him. All labeled Sessions 1 through 9, with the box to Session 5 open and its tape playing on the reel-to-reel.

"It appears Ms. Hobbes is entering a dissociative state again," Doctor David Adams said over the speaker. *"She is rubbing her eyes manically."*

Mike's walkie-talkie sprang to life with the angered voice of Gordon. "Mike, where are you? Come back!"

"Mary?" the doctor continued, then addressed the recorder. *"The subject is rubbing her eyes harder. I think this is her switching to an alternate personality—"*

"Mike!" Gordon barked again over the walkie, sounding more annoyed by the second.

Picking it up, Mike replied on autopilot into the walkie, staring at the spinning reels. "On my way, boss," he mumbled quickly before placing it back on the table.

After a pause and a shrug, Mike leaned over to turn off the player—

"Hello, sir," a young male voice sounded from the speaker.

Mike's finger froze over the stop button. He stared at the reels.

"Hello, Billy," the doctor replied. *"Nice to talk to you again."*

"You as well, sir."

Mike turned his glance down to the tape box for Session 5. He focused on the words. ALTERS: *The Princess, Billy, "Simon."*

"That's Mary?" he muttered in confusion, aghast that the voice of Billy could come from her.

Sure, Princess was just a girl's voice she could have adopted without difficulty.

But this sounded like a real boy.

"Billy, where does Princess live?" the doctor asked.

"In the knee."

Billy's voice was so believably male Mike could not get past that it was Mary Hobbes.

"And where do you live, Billy?" the doctor said.

"I live in the eyes. You know that..."

At the gazebo, Hank sat up on a bench, sunglasses still on, playing his scratch cards.

"Remind me, Billy," the doctor asked. *"Why do you live in the eyes?"*

"Because I-I see everything, sir."

From his seat, Gordon watched, unimpressed, as Mike exited the side door of the building and walked across the grass toward them.

"And where does Simon live, Billy? Can you tell me that?"

Billy did not respond.

"Billy?" the doctor persisted. *"Where does Simon live? I really need you to tell me. Haven't I been kind to you? You know I'm your friend. You can let me know."*

Mike arrived at the gazebo just as Jeff motioned to the yellow document.

"Anyone know what mortified pride is?" Jeff asked. "Says on this thing that three patients were committed to Danvers in 1889 because of 'mortified pride.'"

"Eighteen eighty-nine?" Phil asked, leaning over to look at the paper. "Let me see that." Jeff handed him the old document, and he glanced over the type upon it. "Where'd you find this?"

Jeff shrugged. "Was lyin' under some boxes." He motioned to the paper. "It's intense, some of the shit they just left in this place. Lying about like it was nothin'. The kitchen is filled with scraps of paper, just out in the wind, gatherin' dust. This place probably has a lot of cool stuff just lyin' around."

Hank couldn't help but smile, remembering his own found *cool stuff*, the old coin stash.

As Phil read the piece of paper, Mike sat beside Jeff.

Gordon stared at him. "When Phil calls lunch, Mike," he said gruffly, "it means lunch. No fannying about on your own in there."

"Sorry," Mike said, shrugging off the scolding. "But we got no gaskets. And no gaskets means no work. So, I'll have to pick up more tomorrow at Grossman's if I can't find where ours went."

"Then, take someone with you if you go," Gordon countered. "Can't have you falling through some rotten boards with no one able to hear you screaming."

"That's dark," Jeff exclaimed, smiling.

Phil, still reading the paper in one hand, handed Mike a noodle box and chopsticks with the other. He then read aloud, "Seventeen people were committed here due to disappointed expectations." He laughed. "Hear that one, Henry? Back in those days, they would have committed you."

Jeff laughed. "Wonder what kind of shit you have to do now to get committed nowadays?"

Hank turned his head without any smile and stared up at Phil over the rim of his sunglasses. "Simple answer to that. You gotta kill someone to get thrown in a place like this."

"That won't get you committed, Hank," Gordon replied. "That'll just get you thrown straight to jail, mad or not."

Phil stared right back at Hank, not blinking. "You'll only go to jail *if* you get caught." He then looked down and opened his noodle box, from which steam billowed out.

Hank scoffed. "Nah. Temporary insanity is the way to go. Like John Hinckley. He's not in jail. He's in the nuthouse. Right, Mike?"

"That's not the norm," Mike replied with an unimpressed grimace. He then pulled out his true crime book from his breast pocket. "Madness defense rarely works in most cases. Most people are cognizant of their actions when they murder someone. Homicide, by its nature, implies a motive. Just in the movies, that crap works."

All of the men looked at him in surprise.

"God, Mike. How the hell did you fail law school? You're so knowledgeable," Phil said sarcastically.

The jibe hit its mark as Mike gritted his teeth.

Shaking his head, he removed his chopsticks from their packet and opened his noodle box.

"Yeah, what are you, dude?" Jeff said, trying to join in the mockery. "Some kind of lobotomy or something?" He laughed hysterically at his own joke.

"Jeff, do you even know what the words you are saying mean?" Mike quipped, more amused than annoyed.

Jeff just shrugged, still smiling.

"Are you some kind of lobotomy?" Mike repeated, laughing. "Christ, you're absurd. That's not how you would say the word."

"And you're a poet, and you don't half know it!" Jeff countered quickly.

Mike's smile faltered, as a chilling familiarity swept over him.

Jeff then leaned into Mike, leering like a zombie, letting a little drool dribble from the corner of his mouth. "Loh... bah... toe... me..." he said in a slow drawl.

"Jeff," Gordon said, rolling his eyes in annoyance. "Christ's sake. Mellow out, or I'll call your dad."

Without a word, Mike gently put his noodle box down by his side on the bench, as well as one chopstick. The other, he kept gripped firmly.

In a swift, explosive action, he then grabbed Jeff and

pulled him down on his lap, face up. Trying to squirm out, Jeff laughed nervously, but Mike was significantly stronger.

With a chillingly calm demeanor, Mike held the chopstick and pointed down at Jeff like the Sword of Damocles. "In 1946, Walter Freeman invented the ice-pick method of lobotomies." He then moved the chopstick slowly down, tip first, closer to Jeff's face. "First, you insert a thin metal pipette into the orbitofrontal cortex." Lowering the chopstick nearer, he aimed it toward Jeff's eye.

Jeff stopped squirming as his laughter faded, a fear creeping in, as the chopstick got closer and closer.

"A rapid *push* to penetrate the thin bone and enter the soft tissue of the frontal lobe." Mike lowered the pointed chopstick millimeters away from Jeff's tear duct.

The rest of the crew sat, totally silent, unsure of what was happening.

Jeff was as still as possible, slowly fearing for his own safety but too much of a coward to fight against it.

"Mike," Gordon said, unimpressed, "come on."

"It's alright, Gordon," Mike replied, stone-faced. "It's a quick procedure. A few simple, smooth, up-and-down jerks to sever the lateral hypothalamus, all resulting in a very rapid reduction in emotional stress for our patient." The chopstick hovered closer and closer over Jeff's eye. Mike's hand was perfectly still and in control. "To finish, you then gently slip out the pipette, a dab of antibiotic in the corner of the eye. Total time elapsed. Two minutes.

Only side effect, a black eye. Recommended treatment, sunglasses."

Mike suddenly smiled and let his viselike grip on Jeff go.

With a cheer, Hank applauded the performance. "Bravo, Mike. Bravo."

Jeff sat, bolt upright, brushing himself off, slightly freaked out by what had just happened. "Not funny, Mike."

"Wrong, Jeff. That was fucking funny," Hank corrected.

Phil hadn't paid much attention to this performance; instead, he silently watched Hank.

After lunch, when all of the crew went back to work through the kitchen, a figure stepped quietly into the dark tunnels, looking up at the ceiling as they walked. Sensing the men above them.

"Mike," Hank said as he and Jeff wheeled the tile puller across the kitchen floor. "I may have said it in a dick way before, but I wasn't kidding, you know?"

Mike was crouched at the other end of the room, searching through a crate of tools. He spoke without looking up. "What the hell are you talking about?"

Before he answered, Hank grunted, pushing the tile puller into place over a section of cracked flooring. Then, standing up straight, he turned to Mike with a shrug. "You know, dude, you're way smarter than this job. You should be using your head somewhere, not sweating your lungs out, breathing frickin' asbestos dust."

Mike turned back and glared at Hank, who attempted an apologetic smile at him.

Jeff, looking uneasy between the two men, was stuck in the middle.

"Whatever," Mike said dismissively, standing and turning to walk away. "I gotta get a part from the van. Show Jeff how to operate that thing, would ya? He hasn't listened to me."

Hank quickly grabbed a walkie-talkie from the counter, then called out, "Hey, Mikey?" As Mike turned, Hank smiled and winked. "Don't forget this." He tossed the walkie to Mike, who caught it with ease in one hand.

Without any response, Mike turned and walked out of the kitchen.

Hank, hiding any hurt from Mike's refusal of an apology, just watched him leave, the smile still on his face. "Ever ride a lawnmower before?" he asked loudly.

"Mike tried to compare it to that." Jeff shrugged, looking nervously at the tile puller. "I wasn't so good. Think I blew the fuses, and Mike... Think he hates me 'cos I couldn't get it."

"Well, get back on that horse and give it another go. I have faith in you, hoss." Mike turned and motioned to the machine. "And don't worry about old Mr. Grumpy Pants. He is always like that." Hank's smile grew cockier.

"I'm taking a smoke. You get started on the right side of the room."

"But we just had a break," Jeff complained. "And I... I dunno what I'm doing."

With a shrug, Hank walked over to the boom box and switched it on. The easy listening flowed out soothingly. Turning the dial, he spun through white static and various dull stations—"KR2, The Rock Station! Here to play the heaviest of hits!" blared out.

Jeff stared as Hank turned up the volume, then looked to him. "I think you are reading into it all too much," Hank said. "You gotta use this job just as a job. Don't care if you don't know shit, just bluff it. You need your own whale to focus on." He looked at Jeff's confused expression. "You know what a whale is, Jeff?" Hank asked, carelessly perching himself on a stack of removed asbestos tiles. He took out a cigarette and placed it between his lips.

"Sure, I do, I'm not an idiot. Big thing in the sea."

Hank nodded, lit his cigarette, and took a long drag. With a long exhale, he used his free hand to crack off a piece of asbestos tile. "Aside from the swimming ones. A whale's also a big gambler in a casino," he continued. "And I know a guy who dealt this whale at Foxwoods. After twelve hours, the whale had the house down three hundred grand. He knows he's done all he can. So, he decides to walk away. Before he goes, he drops his car keys in my friend's pocket. Says, 'Keep 'em.'" Hank then looked down at the fragment of tile and crumbled it in a tight fist.

"Yeah? What has that got to do with this?"

Hank smirked. "Guess what those keys were for?"

Jeff shrugged.

"A Porsche 911." He took another drag. "Whale just gave it without a second thought. You see, that was a tip. That's where the money is for people like us. Serving the greedy and rich. That man was a whale. He was the dream client. The dream. The whale is the dream. You need your own whale. We all do."

"What are you sayin'?"

Jeff's confusion was palpable.

"Look at it like this... Miami Casino School grads make sixty-grand salary the first year out. Before tips. Now, tell me, Jeff, what is twenty-five K split five ways? Even *you* can figure that one out."

Jeff nodded. "Five K. What's your point?"

"Just weigh your options, dude." Hank smiled enigmatically. "Stay on this job too long, it'll mess with your head. The stress is the thing." He held up his fist and slowly opened it, releasing the crumbled tile. "You've been here a day, and already, an itty-bitty piece of this may have gotten in to you. It incubates in your lungs, Jeff." His smile dropped. "Tissue begins growing around it. Like a pearl. Like a time bomb. Time you hit thirty, then BOOM!"

Jeff jolted.

"Boom, and you're drowning in your own lung fluid." Hank wiped his dusty hand on his trouser leg.

Jeff, meanwhile, started to look very worried.

"If you're careful." Hank chuckled. "You'll probably make out alright. But one slip-up. One misplaced breath..." He pointed at Jeff with his cigarette between his fingers. "Look, man, you're not even wearing your mask right now." Hank took another drag as Jeff hastily pulled up his mask from around his neck.

"You're not wearing one either," Jeff said, his voice slightly muffled.

Hank just shrugged and took another drag. "I've learned to sublimate my fear. 'Cos I got an exit plan. I got my whale in my sights. See, doesn't always have to be a person. Doesn't have to be gambling. Just has to be that one unattainable thing. The whale. That's how I deal with the stress. I keep my whale in my sights and remember this job isn't my life and that I shouldn't care about the little things. And besides, if I was gonna get anything bad from being on the job, ain't no escaping it now. See, ya gotta have a way of dealing. You think Mike reads all those books for fun? See, he's got a plan. He's got his whale. He's gonna go back, finish law school. Pass the Bar. Get the big juicy cases. Make his dad proud. That dream, that whale, keeps him going. And he'll bolt when the stress gets too intense and the opportunity shows itself."

The back of Gordon's van opened, and Mike hopped in. Ducking to avoid hitting his head on the roof, he moved over to a mini workbench inside, replete with boxes of tools on top. He rummaged around, looking for the part.

Just then, something caught his eye.

Glancing down, he moved a box of wrenches out of the way and saw that, behind it, an unopened bottle of champagne was placed.

"And as for Phil?" Hank laughed aloud. "Phil's not got an exit plan, but boy does he have a way to cope! He's got one hell of a stress reducer. I'm sure you'll smell it on him one day. Maybe even give you some... But he's on his hundredth warning from Gordo about it."

Jeff looked surprised.

"Every time he's caught with any," Hank continued. "It's Phil's last chance. Gordon's got zero tolerance for that stuff. Unless it's Phil, of course. Then he'll lose his shit, threaten to fire him, then forget about it the next day. So, we go on as usual. But it's how Phil copes. His whale isn't as much a whale as an acceptance that he doesn't have one, so he has to find a way to not kill himself."

"So, he smokes weed?" Jeff asked.

"Weed, blow, you name it. He's probably on it." Hank shrugged. "Not a new thing either. Always been like that since the day I met him."

In the gym, Phil followed the cables across the floor toward the exit and peered around nervously. Making sure he was not being watched.

Jeff listened intently. Not sure of how or what to respond.

Hank took another drag, then flicked his ash onto the floor. "Then there's Uncle Gordo... Y'know, if he didn't get this gig, that he'd have to fold H.E.C.?" Noticing Jeff's sudden surprise, Hank nodded. "Yup. And he can't even have an exit plan 'cos fiber is his life. Imagine *that* stress... But let me tell you something, just hope, hope, you got some of his genes, dude! Because Gordo is the zen master of calm. Control with a capital C. Never seen ol' Gordo lose it. Gets pissy at us, sure, but that's all it is. And we deserve what he shouts at us one hundred percent of the time."

In the containment room, Gordon was busy at work, fully masked up with his goggles on.

His mind would normally be solely focused on the job, working out the rest of the schedule in his head. Planning what they needed to do to finish by the deadline—but right here and now? His mind had trouble focusing on anything. His actions were on autopilot.

Hank watched his exhaled smoke dissipate in the room. With brows furrowed, he could not shake a feeling. "Over the past few months, with Gordo... I'm startin' to see the cracks. I worry about him—"

Mike pushed open the double doors and walked back into the kitchen.

Relieved it was not anyone else, Hank continued. "Mikey knows what I'm sayin', eh, Mikey?"

"He's got a baby, though," Jeff said. "Must be a lot to manage."

"Should be the joy of his life, dude." Hank shook his head. "But..."

"Put that out," Mike said, pointing at Hank's cigarette. "And just wait 'til you and Amy have a kid. It's not that easy, y'know?"

Hank burst into laughter. "Me and Amy!? A kid with Amy!? I just fuck her to beat on Phil as well, you know."

Mike frowned in disgust, then shook his head. "Get off your fucking ass and do some work."

Hank stood up, off the pile of tiles. "I'm just sayin', have an exit plan, Jeff." He then stubbed his cigarette out on the floor with the heel of his boot.

"What's *your* plan, then?" Jeff asked.

Hank curled his enigmatic smile again.

"His exit plan's gonna be in a fucking coffin if he doesn't get back to work." Mike sighed. "And I want my bonus! Now, let's get on with it. Get on the puller!"

In a containment room, Gordon staggered over to the small window. He pulled off his goggles and PAPR respirator as sweat dripped down his face.

His breathing was stilted and heavy. His exhaustion was getting the better of him.

Fumbling, he pulled out his cell phone and speed-dialed a number. Waiting for the call to be picked up, he stared blankly out of the window.

His other hand absently mindedly moved up to his ear, and he rubbed it as if it was bothering him.

"Hi... Wendy." He spoke desperately into the phone while he stared at the wooden steps outside the window. "No, please, please don't hang up. Please, just listen... Honey... there's something I want to say... No, I know, I know... but listen to me... Please, just listen... I love you. Believe me. I didn't mean to..."

Directly above Gordon, in the dark attic, a figure turned in the shadows as it heard Gordon speaking from the room below. Indistinct words, but ones that caused the figure to then lie on the bare floorboards, listening in closer.

Gordon hung up his call, wiping a tear. He soon noticed a dark, sticky substance all over his fingers. Quickly, he smeared them on his overalls and looked back out of the window. He tried to steel his resolve after such an emotional call.

Taking a deep breath, he closed his eyes and breathed calmly for a few moments.

Slowly opening them again, he peered out of the window for the second time through the polythene. He noticed something move by some trees.

Looking more intently, he saw Phil talking to two young men, who both wore bandanas. He gesticulated nervously.

Gordon frowned. The memory of his call dragged away as his emotions turned into annoyance.

Later that night, as darkness engulfed the daylight, the gates of the Danvers State Hospital opened wide, and a battered Chrysler drove up the winding road for the second time that day.

Parking behind the machine shop to the left of the complex, hidden from plain view, the door to the car opened as a few used scratch cards fell to the ground.

Grabbing the flashlight from his glove compartment, Hank then picked up his Walkman and put the headphones over his ears. Slamming play, he smiled as the song blared in his ears, eclipsing his secret nervousness.

Grabbing a leather satchel from the passenger seat, he then got out of the car and took in a sharp, deep breath.

"Okay. Let's do this thing," he muttered, slamming the car door shut. "Baby needs a new pair of shoes."

He couldn't hide his excitement nor his trepidation. "Here we go. Let's not fuck this up."

Walking through this hospital alone at night would normally scare any person, but Hank's mind was focused on his coins. The things that could be key to getting out of his dull life.

Propelled by nervous energy, he walked by a rusty gurney, humming along softly to his music to dispel the surrounding creepiness.

As he reached the gym and the steps down to the tunnel, he turned his flashlight on and descended slowly.

Only a few minutes later, he yanked the brick pieces and eagerly scooped handfuls of coins out into his leather satchel. More and more came out until his hand reached something further, something different. He pulled out a set of old silver-framed glasses.

Looking at them curiously, with music still playing loudly in his ears, he mumbled, "What the hell?"

Quickly, he threw his arm deeper into the hole. He dug around as far as he could reach. After a few moments, he pulled out a collection of watches, rings, brooches—some with paper ID tags still attached.

Switching off his music, he focused all his attention

onto this. He then opened a random brooch with his free hand, and a daguerreotype of a corseted woman stared back out. Shaking his head with a shrug, he just threw it into his satchel.

Reaching back into the wall, he then brought out a handful of used gold teeth fillings and a couple of glass eyes.

With a chuckle, he continued until his hand found a small, oblong mahogany case, complete with gold leaf script upon it that stated *Dr. W Freeman, Orbitoclasts.*

Holding the flashlight in his mouth, Hank then used his hands to open the small case. With a creak, the lid opened up, revealing two medical tools, both silver, set in purple velvet. They were long and thin, like pointed chopsticks. Picks with a gripped handle at one end, lobotomy picks.

Ten minutes later, Hank walked back through the tunnel, flashlight in one hand, a satchel brimming with found treasure in the other.

His music was back on, loudly playing into his ears, and wore a self-satisfied grin larger than he had been able to don for years.

Ahead in the tunnel, he then caught sight of something blue on the floor, something round standing out from the brown of the dirt.

Stopping, he peered down and saw a new-looking plastic jar of peanut butter. One that did not have any dirt upon it. Kicking it, he could see that someone had scraped it clean. The little that was left in there looked black in this light.

Glancing around, Hank suddenly felt an uncontrollable pang of nerves. Turning off his music yet again, he removed the headphones and moved the flashlight. Scanning the tunnels surrounding him.

He felt something wasn't right. Probably his nerves, he thought.

Creeeeeaak.

The noise caused Hank to spin with a panic. His light shone brightly yet dissolved into the muddy darkness ahead of him, unable to pierce it.

For a second, he breathed, staring. Motes of airborne dust sparkled in the light like stars. But he saw no shapes in the darkness. No people waiting to take his treasure. No movement at all. Just silence.

Shaking off his thoughts, he turned back to leave.

Cooooo.

Turning toward the void, creeped out again, he shouted, "Who the fuck's there?"

He aimed the light down the tunnel, anxiously hoping nothing was looking back. Squinting, he tried to focus on what may be making the noises. But all he saw was just seamless darkness. An opaque murk. Wait...

He squinted more, focusing his flashlight on one spot farther down the tunnel. A spot that shifted.

Just before the flashlight's beam gave into the darkness beyond... was... a shape.

Gulping, Hank stared. Was his mind playing tricks on him?

Slowly, very slowly. The shape in the darkness started to get bigger, much bigger.

Sprinting down the tunnel, with his flashlight dancing in front of him, Hank's heart thudded while he tried to find his escape. His loot jangled as his legs pounded the dirt below, the satchel swinging from side to side.

He tossed a frantic look over his shoulder before banking right into another tunnel—one that the crew hadn't been into yet.

He raced by piles of moldy clothes, clots of old cobwebs matted onto the low arched ceiling, puddles of brown water, as well as bones of dead things long trapped down there.

Compared to the rest of the decaying hospital, this tunnel was the worst place he had seen. An absolute hell, made worse by his panic. But he had no time to dwell. He barreled farther on, hoping to find a staircase.

Suddenly, he skidded to a halt with a gasp and was met with a dead end.

Spinning as a noise flapped closer, Hank instinctively raised his hands in defense, ready to face his certain annihilation against—a gray pigeon. One that burst at him from the darkness and fluttered over his head before turning back around.

Coooo.

As the bird disappeared around a corner, Hank, dazed, tried to quell his panic with a nervous guffaw. Relieved, he took a series of huge breaths. "Fuck me," he managed to utter. "Chill out, Hank. Just a bird."

His flashlight scanned over the tunnel around him. It illuminated an exit sign to his left.

He smiled, relieved.

Chapter 6

Wednesday

A ceramic tile snapped and buckled under the pressure of the crowbar that levered it off. As it fell from the wall to the floor, the crowbar moved on to the next piece. As it did, a smattering of thin white dust drifted into the air, released from decades of being sealed behind the ceramic slabs.

Phil, fully covered in his hazmat suit, mask, and goggles, was in full swing, focused and working like a machine. Since his early arrival, being the first on the site, he had not stopped. After another night propping up a bar, he fought the dull ache in his mind as well as ghosts of his misfortune, with exception and sweat. It was a new day, and it would be a better day, he hoped.

This room, one of the larger rooms in Ward C, was just like the others, fully draped in plastic sheets, with a negative air vacuum humming away in the corner.

Gordon, as indistinguishable as Phil in his own hazmat gear, stood halfway up a ladder, busily making good progress on pulling down the ceiling tiles.

Both worked away in silence, locked in their own minds. This was the way they always operated in the past, with all chit-chat and gossiping saved for breaks. Both men enjoyed just getting in, getting it done, and getting out at the end of the day. This was how they functioned best.

That day, though, both men could sense something was off with the other. Neither could place their finger on what it was, but it was something...

Across the complex in the gym, also fully suited up, Mike watched as Jeff finally managed to drive the tile puller throughout the room. The machine effortlessly crunched its way over a patch of tiles, its forward blade ripping through them with ease. Much easier than the ones they removed in the kitchen.

Finally! Mike thought, relieved that Jeff was just slow on the uptake and not a total lost cause. He finally had listened to Mike's directions after three days.

Beneath the gym, there was no sound except the electrical hum of utility lights that streaked along the length of the tunnels.

Outside the morgue, the hole that Hank had made

still lay broken. On the dirt floor in front of it, a couple of coins lay, left in the hurried events of the previous night's heist.

In the morgue itself, in the dark, something moved, something that carried with it an air of anger.

Two hours later, drenched in sweat, Phil gulped down bottled water. Standing on top of the flat roof of the female wing, he anxiously glanced at Gordon, who was sitting on a chair, cell phone in hand, frustratedly waiting for a call to pick up.

After a few moments, Gordon looked at Phil and shook his head. "Damn machine's not even on." He sighed, hung up the call, and put his cell in his pocket.

Phil rolled his eyes, then looked at his watch. "The man's a liability," he moaned. "Bet this is just to piss me off."

Just as he spoke, Mike and Jeff walked from the roof access door to join them for a few moments' rest.

"I'm guessing Hank's still pulling a disappearing act?" Mike asked, pulling off his gloves.

"Maybe he's at Amy's?" Jeff proffered, to which Mike threw him a stern look to stop talking. "What? He *might* be."

Shrugging off the comment, Phil shook his head. "Better check all your tools. Make sure he hasn't stolen any to pawn."

Gordon thought for a beat. "I'll get her number," he

said, taking his cell phone out again and started dialing the operator. He waited until he heard a call pick up. "I need the number for Amy Girardi in—"

Phil strode over and grabbed the phone from Gordon's hand. "Jesus, let me do it. I know her number. At this point, I don't even care if she wants me to call or not."

Gordon and the others could only watch silently as Phil hung up the operator call, then jabbed his fingers into the keypad, dialing his ex's number from memory.

"All this time, and I know her number better than I know my own." Phil turned away from the men, then pressed the dial button.

Mike turned to Gordon with raised eyebrows, to which Gordon just shook his head.

"Amy? Hi, it's me." As Phil spoke into the phone, his anger and annoyance fell away. His tone became kind and apologetic. "How ya been? Yeah, I know I said I wouldn't call, but it's important... It's about Hank... Can I... ? Well, I'm about to tell you..."

Jeff smiled in amusement at the call and glanced at Phil and Gordon.

Neither of whom found any humor in this.

"What?" Phil asked in shock, and a long pause followed. He turned around and looked at Gordon with a wide-eyed stare. "Hank did what? No... I have no idea what you're talking about. He just left?"

Gordon watched Phil intently as his hand absentmindedly rubbed his ear.

"Really?... Well, that's awful." Phil said into the phone with a smile, unable to conceal his delight. "I'm really sorry to hear that, Amy... What? No, I'm serious... What?!... I don't care if you don't fuckin' believe me. I— oh, fuck you, too, A—"

A sudden silence fell as Phil paused before moving the phone from his ear. Taking a deep breath in, Phil handed the phone back to Gordon with an appreciative nod.

"What she say?" Gordon asked.

"So, apparently, last night, ol' Hank goes over to her place, starts loading all his stuff into his car, the stereo he loaned her, his CDs and shit." He couldn't help a small chuckle escape. "He told Amy he's 'going to pick up his meal ticket' and fly off to Miami... to that casino school he wouldn't shut up about."

Mike suddenly burst into hearty laughter. "What? You're kidding."

"What meal ticket?" Jeff asked.

Phil shrugged nonchalantly, with a self-satisfied feeling of victory. "I warned her he was a fucker. She didn't believe me. Well, now she knows." Looking down at the ground for the moment, he mumbled, "Got what she deserved I guess."

Trying to process everything, Gordon stood and walked a few feet away, looking out across the grounds of the hospital from the high vantage point.

"Mike," Jeff asked, looking suddenly, "you think he scored on a scratch? That lucky fuck!"

"Who knows?" Mike sighed, still chuckling. "And at this point, who cares? He wants to go, so be it."

Phil stepped over to Gordon, who was at the roof's edge.

"I get he wanted to go, never made that a secret or anything," Gordon mused. "But why leave without saying anything? Anything? He had two days' work to be paid for. Not like him to leave any money."

Phil, strangely unfazed, put a hand on Gordon's shoulder. "I know you think I'm saying it just because of Amy, but he was always unreliable, Gordon." He moved in closer and spoke at a more personal volume. "Listen, fuck him. He's history. He wants to go, so be it..."

Gordon, though, was not really listening. His focus was on something he had looked at before from one of the hospital windows, the wooden steps that led down to the woods. "Something's not right about this."

"Hank going AWOL?" Phil replied. "I don't know. I think it makes total sense."

Still in his aimed stare, Gordon spoke softly. "We need five guys for this job. Or we may as well just quit now... Hank leaving doesn't make sense. He wanted money—he wouldn't just leave it. He would tell me he quit and ask for the pay."

"Gordo, I'm on it. It's all good!" Phil smiled, turning to Mike. "Yo, Mikey, call Craig McManus. You got his number still?"

Mike nodded.

"Hope he's still up for the job," Phil said, rubbing the back of his neck. Noticing Gordon's cold-eyed stare toward the wooden steps. "What is it?"

"I have to ask you, Phil. And please don't lie to me," Gordon said, nodding to the tree line ahead. "Who were those guys you were talking to down there?"

Caught off guard, Phil swallowed hard as Gordon turned and looked him dead in the eye.

"You know what I'm talking about," Gordon chided. "I saw you. Yesterday. Down there. You and those kids."

"Are you kidding me, Gordo?" Phil stumbled over his words with a nervous laugh.

Gordon, not blinking, moved in closer. His voice lower and sterner, slowing down to a crawl, deliberately emphasizing each word. "Phil. What were you talking to them about?"

Quickly glancing at the others, Phil turned back to Gordon. "What is this?" he said in a hushed tone. "What do you want?"

"You tell me, Phil." Gordon didn't break eye contact and didn't blink. "What. Is. This?"

"Are you questioning my performance here?"

Gordon, with his eyes kept dead level on Phil, almost snarled. "I don't know. Should I be? Now, tell me what you spoke to them about. Something ain't right here, and it's smelling like you had something to do with it?"

"I'm not doing this," Phil said, aghast, slowly turning away. Looking at Mike, he shouted, "Christ's sake, Mike.

Call Craig, goddammit! Now!" He waved to shoo them away. "Jeff, you, too. Break's over! Back to work."

As Phil was about to storm off, Gordon bared his teeth in a grimace, lunged at him, grabbed his collar, and swung him back around.

With eyes blazing, fierce and dangerous, this was not the Gordon that Phil nor any of the men had seen before.

His bottom lip trembled. He tried to vocalize his anger. His hand clenched on Phil's collar like a vise, leaning him over the walled edge of the roof.

With their faces inches apart, Phil was more shocked than scared.

"What? You gonna hit me, Gordon?" he shouted. "What the fuck is wrong with you, huh?"

Gordon's eyes burst wide with a sudden terror of realization, as his jaw dropped in shock. He saw what he was doing and felt a horror that he had no control over stopping it before it happened.

Abruptly letting go of Phil's collar, Gordon was left staring at his hands in shock as Phil pulled away, straightening his shirt angrily.

Mike and Jeff watched, speechless, as Phil stormed off, soon followed by Gordon.

When they were alone on the roof, Jeff turned to Mike. "What the hell was that?" he asked, freaked out. "I've never seen my uncle like that."

"I could lie, but I got no damn idea."

Out of view, hidden behind the machine shop, Hank's battered Chrysler still sat.

Storming into a patient's seclusion room, Phil tried to contain his rage. Grunting loudly in frustration, he paused, staring at the collage of images across the walls, the images that had fascinated him not so long ago. In an explosion of anger, he violently smashed into the rotten wall with his boot. Kicking at the brittle plaster again and again. Letting out a furious roar with each hit.

Underneath a big peeling A on a gloomy stairwell, Gordon sat awkwardly on the bottom step. Under a string of yellow caution tape.

He was spent. Exhausted.

Tentatively touching his left thigh with his palm, he winced in pain. But that pain wasn't alone; in fact, his whole body ached. Even his eyeballs felt sore.

Staring at his trembling hands, he, again, noticed the dark, sticky substance over them. Rubbing the muck on his overalls, he shook his head, then dropped his gaze despondently.

His glance traced the floor, at all the dirt and rubbish that glimmered in the sunlight coming in from the grated windows from high up the staircase behind him. His gaze set on a light patch of powder that had fallen from a crumbling ceiling tile down onto the floor.

Imprinted in that powder, almost perfectly, a footprint.

The rest of the morning spun by in a daze for the abatement crew. Gordon was nowhere to be seen. Phil worked alone. Jeff and Mike resumed the gym floor tile removal. Barely a word was spoken by anyone until lunchtime.

"Let him work it off his own way," Mike said, sitting on a bench in the gazebo. "He's got a right to be pissed. It's his business on the line, not just our bonuses." In his hand, he read the yellow hospital commitment document Jeff had found the day before.

Finishing a sandwich, Phil was sitting next to him, looking agitated.

Meanwhile, Jeff was in his own world, quietly perched on an opposite bench. In his hand, he held a pile of fresh scratch cards and was avidly scraping away at them. Hoping for any kind of miracle.

"D'you think I do a bad job here, Mike?" Phil asked, not really wanting an honest answer.

"Course not," Mike replied. "You know you do good."

"This job used to be fun, right?" Phil sighed despondently. "Good, solid gigs. Joking around, beers after work. We were a family. Now it's just..." He looked up across the grass and along the long expanse of the hospital wing. "Is it all even worth it anymore?" he asked softly.

"Never mind that," Mike said, changing the subject. "According to this, in 1891, 'twelve were committed for uncontrolled passion'—now ain't that a bitch? Sent to the loony bin for fuckin' a lot!"

Phil did not want to lose the subject and blanked Mike's input. "Ever since Emma was born, Gordon..."

Mike then turned to Phil with an annoyed glare.

Noticing, Phil threw his hands up in frustration. "What? You know it's why we lost the last two gigs. He was too tired. He overbid. He fucked us. I barely ate those months. One week, I could barely afford gas. Had to get a temp job hauling trash. You think he cared about *that*? No. His focus was forced by Wendy away from us."

"Forced? Gordon loves being a father, Phil," Mike said, trying to counter Phil's rising temper. "You know that."

"Maybe now he does, yeah. But we both know he never wanted that kid before. On the job, he very much let it be known. It was all Wendy's idea."

Mike stood, having enough of Phil's rant, folding the yellow document and putting it back in the breast pocket of his overalls. "Just because you say you don't want something doesn't mean you don't want it. Okay?"

Jeff glanced up from his scratch cards, listening to the conversation unfold.

"I thought I didn't want to be a lawyer six years ago, so I quit," Mike continued. "Now I'm thinking, why the hell not? I gotta have something else—"

"Mike," Phil said, clearly affronted by Mike's opposition. "You shuck fiber for a living. Jesus, who're you kidding? A lawyer? Just stick to the lane you are good at."

Turning, Mike held his tongue.

"Anyhow," Phil continued, "the stress of the kid, it's messing with his head. And messing with our jobs. He should've axed Hank months ago and would have done it if he was the old Gordon."

Mike, without replying, walked away from the conversation and toward the hospital.

"Hey, where're you going?" Phil called out.

"Taking a leak," Mike called back in a monotone.

"Well, you got twenty-five, then get back at it," Phil replied.

Jeff sank back into his scratch cards, hoping for a win, even more than before.

After the men had gone back to work, and when the coast was clear outside, Gordon made his way over to the wooden steps that had caught his attention for so long.

Descending its rotten wooden slats, he soon found himself on an overgrown pathway, littered either side with dead trees and old, rusty lampposts.

In a daze, his mouth half open, he looked like a broken man. His limp, worse than it had been, was very evident in his step.

Past the outline of dead foliage and trees, the further he walked, life seemed to emerge as if it were far enough from the hospital to survive. Flower bushes soon bloomed, and green clumps of grass grew out brightly. What was a seemingly dead woodland from the hospital was, in fact, brimming with life.

As if straight from a romantically pastoral oil painting, Gordon walked by a large patch of open, verdant grass. Upon which, an old, rusty tractor sat idle and forgotten. The rays of the sun fell down upon it in an orange haze.

Finding himself by a small stone wall, Gordon slowed. He listened to the twitter and buzz of birds and insects that filled the air. He looked around at the beautiful serene scene but felt terribly alone.

Leaving Jeff to continue ripping up the gym's floor tiles, Mike had slinked off back down into the tunnels, into the staff library, closing its rickety wooden door behind him.

Determinedly thumbing through a large box of patient record files, he scanned the names on the corner tags of each file, with patients' surnames typed on a small label: Hibbert, Hinton, Hiscox, Hoad... Hobbes.

Hobbes, Mary.

As he read the tag, Mike gleefully smiled. He slid the thick file out of the box and looked at the typed sticker on the front cover.

HOBBES, MARY

Extreme Patient.
Diagnosis: Dissociative Identity Disorder

And a few blank lines beneath that, in big bold, underlined type, read:

<u>DECEASED #444.</u>

Gordon had his cellphone placed to his ear, waiting for an answer to his call. Around him, the sounds of nature quietened to nothing, no birds, no insects. Just an eerie, claustrophobic silence.

Through a thick mess of overgrown grass and reeds, he walked, listening intently to the call.

Just a few steps ahead, a small concrete post jutted out of the ground. Without thinking, he sat, resting on it for a second. Looking up to the sky, he desperately fought the tears that threatened to break free.

"Hi... it's me..." His voice quickly cracked. "No, please. Don't hang up on me, please. *Please*."

No more than twenty feet from where he stood, a small metal sign sat at the entrance to the meadow that read *DSH Cemetery*.

Around him, through the thick grass, Gordon did not notice that the concrete post he rested on was not alone. There were dozens littered throughout this meadow. Posts around three foot tall each, with raised brass numbers affixed to their tips.

"We have to figure this out," Gordon pleaded as a tear streaked down his stubbly cheek. "We need to work it out, baby... Please... I know..." His words suddenly caught in his throat as his upset began to overtake him.

"I don't know why," he blubbered. "It was stupid... Can you forgive me, honey... Please, can you forgive me?"

Beneath him, he did not notice the three brass numbers of the post he rested on, *444*.

"Hey, Uncle Gordon?" a voice called in the distance.

Gordon did not hear anything. "I just want to come home," he said weakly into the phone.

Walking into the cemetery, Jeff made his way over to Gordon, who was facing away. "Gordon?" he shouted louder.

Jolted into the present by his nephew's call, Gordon quickly hung up the cell and put it in his pocket. Turning to see Jeff approaching, he seemed dazed, as if woken from a dream. Focusing on the surrounding reality, the sounds of nature began to rush back into his ears.

"Sorry, didn't see you were on a call." Jeff greeted him with a smile.

Gordon forced a smile back, but it was a poor attempt. "No problem." He motioned to a concrete post next to him numbered *443*. "Take a load off."

Jeff happily sat on top of the grave marker, then turned to his uncle. "I wanted to speak to you on your own, to say thanks for giving me the job—I know my dad probably asked you to give me a break, but—"

"Your dad?" Gordon replied, amused, clawing his emotions to being back under his control and erecting a mask to hide them. "Not at all. I really do need you, Jeff. It's hard crewing up now. Y'know... the Big Dig. I need people I can trust. And you're kin. Kin are always there for each other."

"Well, I just wanted to let you know. I'll work my ass off double-time for you. Okay? I'll work for three men." He smiled wider. "So, no need for any stress. Hank was a dick anyhow. Besides, things'll work out. They always do."

Gordon smiled. "I know they do. It just gets a bit much sometimes." He turned and looked out at the trees surrounding the meadow, feeling the serenity of the place.

"Was that Aunt Wendy?" Jeff asked.

"What?"

"Aunt Wendy, who you were just talking to?" Jeff motioned to Gordon's pocket. "On the phone?"

Gordon, a bit confused, slowly nodded.

"How's she doing? Haven't seen her since the christening."

"She's doing..." Gordon chose his next words carefully. "Okay. Hard with a baby, you know?"

Jeff laughed. "Oh, my dad got his photos from the christening back last week..." His laughing grew louder. "Boy, Emma looked pretty pissed at the priest."

Gordon smiled bitterly. "I don't think she liked the water too much."

Jeff was happy he managed to thank his uncle and that he could hide the fact that he didn't want to be working this job at all. But his was the path of the easy life, so not pissing off his father—or uncle, for that matter—was what he had to do.

An empty tape box lay on the countertop: *Session 7*.

"Why are you crying, Billy?" the voice of Dr. David Adams asked over the reel-to-reel machine's speaker.

"Because I miss Danny. We used to play all the time." Billy sobbed.

Even through the upset, Mary's alter was solid in their presence. The voice unwavering. The personality defined.

As the session's recording played, Mike had Mary's file open in front of him. The orange light bulb in the room pulsed rhythmically like a heartbeat as the electricity flowed through it.

He looked down at a black-and-white family photo. The white label at the bottom read:

Circa: 1960.
(L-R) Frank Hobbes (Father, 38). Nancy Hobbes (Mother, 36). Mary Hobbes (Daughter, 10). Danny Hobbes (Brother, 15).

"Why won't you tell me what happened to Danny?" the doctor implored. *"I know you saw what happened, Billy..."*

"I don't want to scare Princess and Mary, sir."

Billy's sobs broke. He sniffed loudly.

"You won't scare anyone, don't worry," the doctor reassured calmly.

"I won't do it! They're good girls," Billy replied.

Mike focused on the image of Mary in her family portrait. Grinning out cutely, complete with long ponytails.

He turned the pages through more photos, photos of her youth, playful and happy.

"Well, maybe Simon would like to tell me what happened that day?"

Mike looked up at the spinning tape, enraptured by Simon's name being spoken.

"No! No!" Billy cried, scared. *"Simon is asleep, sir! You never want to wake him. Never ever, ever."*

"Why not, Billy?" the doctor asked, confused.

"You know perfectly well why!" Billy's words were filled with genuine panic. *"It's why Mary's here at this hospital!"*

Turning to the next page, Mike was confronted by a photo of an older Mary Hobbes. The patient Mary Hobbes. Complete with a shaved head, sporting the twisted, tortured grimace of someone suffering a severe mental illness.

"Billy, Mary needs to know what happened," the

doctor said, calmly and evenly. *"She needs to remember, or we can't help her. Would you tell me so I can tell her?"*

"NO!" Billy screamed defiantly. *"I WON'T LET HER KNOW! NO! NO! NO!"*

Mike breathed more stiltedly. He began to feel uneasy while listening to the recording.

"Okay, fine, then just help me wake Simon," the doctor asked again. *"As you won't help me, I want to speak to Simon, Billy! I must do so!"*

In the decontamination room, with the workday now coming to a close, Phil stepped out of the portable shower. A towel wrapped around his waist.

Gordon, still hazmat suited, stood on the other side of the room, hanging his mask up on a hook. He glanced over to Phil, who was walking in.

After a day of covering not only his but Hank's work as well, Phil felt too tired to argue anymore.

Amid the awkward silence, they nodded at each other.

Gordon then sat on the bench, staring at the floor.

"You gonna shower?" Phil asked, making some small talk. "Shouldn't be going home without washing that crap off. You taught me that."

After a pause, still staring downward, Gordon sounded ashamed. "What's the stupidest thing you ever did, Phil?"

His voice was quiet.

141

Struck by the abruptness of the question, Phil froze.

Gordon looked at him with a desperate, imploring look.

"I-I don't know, Gordo," Phil replied. "Maybe agreeing to go work for you," he joked with a kind smile.

Gordon couldn't help but smirk bitterly.

Phil sat next to him. "Or that time we lost the keg on the 95 when it rolled off the pickup. Almost totaled that old dear driving the Civic." He chuckled. "That one was a doozy."

"I..." Gordon said, struggling with words. "I-I hit Wendy, Phil."

He sounded shocked at his own words.

"You did *what*?"

Gordon almost smiled at the absurdity of the situation. "It's my 'stupidest thing.'" He covered his face with his hands and rubbed hard. "I just wanted to celebrate getting the job. You know how much we need this."

Phil nodded, not knowing what to say or do. He could only listen intently to Gordon's confession.

"She was cooking dinner at home, waiting for me," Gordon recalled with a smile. "Ziti or something... I think. And I kinda snuck up behind her. I gave her flowers..." His smile quickly dropped. "She turned." His brow furrowed hard. "Dunno how, but the boiling water on the stove knocked over." As he spoke, he heard the clanging deep in his mind. "Went all over my leg..." His memory played out in his mind's eye like a movie. "The dog starts barking. Then Emma starts screaming." He winced, recalling her cries.

Pausing for a moment, Gordon's shoulders sank. "God. We're both so exhausted." He turned to Phil, beseeching. "I lost it. But only for a second. It was all a blur, y'know? I barely remember doing it. But I did it." He looked confused, picturing himself standing in front of his wife. "I know I did it."

"It's alright, Gordo," Phil said reassuringly, putting one hand on his shoulder.

"Was just a little slap, I think. Barely anything. Not even left a mark. But Wendy..." He remembered the look of horror on her face, and his fell into confusion. "For her, I may as well have broken her nose." He paused for a moment. "Let me put it this way, I haven't been sleeping at home the past few days."

"Where've you been staying?" Phil asked. "You could have stayed at mine, you know?"

"Motel," Gordon said. "She's at her sister's. I've been calling. She's coming around, I think." He took a deep breath. "But, God, I miss her. And Emma... I do. I can't believe I became *that* guy. That asshole guy who beats his wife."

"Stay at mine," Phil offered.

Gordon managed a small smile but shook his head. "Don't tell the other guys, okay? I'll be fine."

Phil nodded.

"And listen," Gordon continued, "go ahead and call

Craig. See if he's still in. You're right. We need him. We need him bad if we are gonna get through this on time."

Phil held out his hand. Gordon took it with an appreciative yet small smile.

"By the way, those kids you asked about?" Phil said. "They were just some graffiti punks. I was telling them to get lost, or I'd sic security on them."

"I know." Gordon nodded, knowing full well that it was a lie and that they were there to supply Phil's habit.

A lie they were both happy to tell each other in this moment.

As the midnight hour struck, the towering monolith of the hospital was silhouetted against a purple-black sky, illuminated by a full moon.

Each of the rooms inside, from the kitchen to the decontamination room to the containment areas to the tunnels, were too dark and empty.

Empty except for the figure that walked through the shadows.

Outside the building, Gordon's van was still parked up. The blue light from its radio illuminated Gordon's face as he sat in the driver's seat.

Dressed in boxers and a T-shirt, he sat with his eyes closed.

On the radio, a talk show therapist was speaking to a patient guest.

"Why Charlene?" the therapist asked. *"Why didn't you leave him?"*

"I was—I was afraid," Charlene replied.

"Afraid? This brute had insulted you, threatened you. He had HIT you!" The radio therapist paused for a second. When Charlene didn't reply, he continued. *"Earth to Charlene, hello! The healthy response to a dangerous situation is to be afraid. Run away! It's called the survival instinct! What did you do, Charlene?"*

Charlene began crying. *"I-I-I stayed."*

"Do enjoy pain, Charlene?"

Gordon wasn't listening to the show. He was deep asleep. His eyes moved rapidly under their lids as his dreams twisted into nightmares. Frozen images of the christening spun through his sleeping mind... Wendy smiling. Emma in his arms. His proud parents. Happy family. Happy times.

"I said, do you enjoy your pain?" the radio therapist repeated.

Suddenly, in Gordon's dream, a pot clattered onto the floor, its metallic lid falling away and spinning like a whirring coin across the tile, pushing away any happiness into the blackness of his subconscious.

The whirring pot lid echoed as flashes appeared of Hank scraping a scratch card, replaced by Mike holding a chopstick over Jeff's eye.

The whirring then grew louder and louder, and his dream turned away from memory—to a new scene, where the image of Mike looked up straight at the dreaming Gordon with a sick, cruel smile plastered on his face.

The image was quickly replaced by one of Jeff reading from the yellow paper. He, too, broke with a memory and looked up straight at the dreaming Gordon —with the same sick, cruel smile.

The scenes spun faster through Gordon's nightmare.

Phil, as he was, taking the small packet from the two kids. Then the reality twisted as all three turned to glare at the dreaming Gordon, each with identically horrific smiles.

The whirring grew louder and louder, becoming a deafening drumroll, as the image switched in his mind to a pair of unknown bloody hands.

The sound of the spinning metal lid screeched to an abrupt halt, ending with a clamorous bang and a bloodcurdling female scream.

In the van, Gordon bolted awake with a gasp, ripped from his sleep by the terrible dream. Confused and disoriented. He scanned his surroundings. His hands were trembling and his breathing shallow. He looked down at his thigh illuminated by the radio's glow. It was one big infected, pus-dripping burn blister. It throbbed with searing ferocity and was a pain that Gordon had trouble ignoring.

Reaching over to the passenger seat, next to the open

half-drunk bottle of champagne, he grabbed a plastic container of antibiotic powder.

After taking off the child-safe lid, he dribbled some powder over the wound. As soon as it hit, the pain intensified for a few moments, and he let out a pained cry as spittle flew from his mouth. A cry that spiraled down into an uncontrollable flood of tears.

Moving along a darkened corridor on an upper floor of the hospital, a pair of lights beamed.

Two young men crept along, both wearing bandanas, the same ones who spoke to Phil the day before. The ones that supplied him with what he needed.

One was smoking a joint, while the other drew a large penis on the wall with a yellow spray-paint can.

"I christen this ship," the spray-painting one said, standing back and admiring his work, "The USS Dickballs!"

The one smoking the joint chuckled loudly. "You forgot the balls," he said, pointing to the graffiti.

With a shrug, the spray-painting one took his can and corrected the work, complete with hairs and veins. "Better?" he asked his friend.

Before the other one could answer, a sudden movement a few meters down the corridor caused them to fall silent and stare. The one with a joint coughed up his hit as the figure in the shadows moved closer to them.

"What the fuck?" was all the spray-painting one could say before both screamed in unison.

They scrambled away down the corridor in panic, both of the mind that they would not return.

In his van, Gordon could not stop his tears nor stop the pain burning in his thigh. He did not see the two young men with bandanas flee the Kirkbride, both pale as ghosts.

Nor did he see the figure look down on him from one of the third-floor windows.

Chapter 7

Thursday

Muted early morning light washed through the poly-covered windows of the latest containment area. Its polythene walls billowed in and out rhythmically like a lung, as a breeze drifted in from a nearby open window.

Sitting in his car in the hospital parking lot, Phil meticulously licked the paper of a joint he had freshly rolled. Carefully twisting one end, he smelled the length of the joint deeply, savoring its skunk-like odor for a few long seconds. Eagerly pressing in the car lighter, he delicately closed the ziplock bag of weed on his lap, cautious not to waste a single strand.

Hearing an engine, he glanced in the rearview mirror and saw Gordon's van approaching through the gates.

"Typical, seven on the dot every morning except this fucking one," he muttered, stashing the joint in his shirt pocket and shoving the bag of weed into his glove compartment.

"Guessed you'd be here early again," Gordon greeted Phil, getting out of his van, carrying two coffee cups. "Brought you a brew."

Closing his car door behind him, Phil smiled and took the offered cup, hiding any annoyance at being disturbed. "Thanks, boss. Guess we both didn't get any sleep... again."

Gordon shrugged, taking a sip of coffee. "Five more days, then I'll sleep for a year."

"Tried calling last night but couldn't get through," Phil said.

"Oh?"

"Yeah, wanted to say so you can rest your mind Craig's all in. He'll meet us here tomorrow morning and do the full weekend. Should really help. The guy is fast." He looked to Gordon for a reaction, but instead, he found him staring out at the rising sun.

"Hey, how you doing, Gordon?" Phil asked quietly. "You speak to Wendy?"

Gordon didn't even look back, but he heard the question. "I just want to go home, Phil," he said, still heartbroken. "I just want to go home."

10:30 a.m., Phil's first chance to be alone.

150

Hiding out on the roof, he took a desperate drag on his joint. Taking hit after hit in quick succession—as if he was psyching himself up for something—he then held a full lungful of smoke in for as long as he could before letting it puff out slowly between his lips.

He relished every second and smiled like he had no more stress in his life. But just as quickly as his other stresses went, Gordon's problems came to the forefront of his mind.

For the next ten minutes, he did not exist in the blissful state that he normally would.

His paranoia and anxiety grew with each puff.

He hit her, he mused, eating more angrily. *He fucking hit her?*

In his gear, it was Jeff's second day on the tile puller, and he had almost mastered it. Easily ripping up tile by tile, it was as if he had been doing it for years. Driving the machine along the edge of the gym, he nodded to the music emanating from his boom box.

Mike stood by the cable box, smiling under his mask, impressed. "Nice one, Princess," he mumbled to himself.

As Jeff turned the puller away from him, Mike carefully wrapped his boot around the orange cable that led down the steps and into the equipment annex. With a strong and very much unnoticed tug, the cord went taut, then came out of the breaker box far below. The music and tile puller's power cut off in an instant.

"You gotta be kidding me!" Mike exclaimed loudly, acting the best he could.

"What the—" Jeff shouted, turning over his shoulder to Mike. "It wasn't me, man. I swear it wasn't!"

Mike raised his hand, palm up. "'S'okay, probably the plug coming out again. It's been doing that a lot." He shrugged. "I'll go try and sort it so it stays fixed. Be as quick as I can, but take thirty just in case."

As he started to walk over to the stairs and to the tunnel, Phil entered, making a beeline for Mike.

"Mike?" Phil asked, unable to tell who was who from their masks.

Mike nodded, grumbling silently behind the mask, annoyed at being interrupted with his plan to disappear to the library.

"Take a break with me for a sec, would ya?" Phil asked.

"Can't," Mike said, mask and goggle still on. "I gotta take a look at the plug downstairs. Keeps coming out. Probably have to replace—"

Phil shook his head. "Let mullethead get to that. I need to talk to you."

"He can't. He's got nycto—"

"Now, c'mon." Phil wasn't playing. He turned to Jeff. "Sack up, go down there, and sort it out. That's not a request!"

Mike, with little choice, followed Phil out of the room, leaving Jeff alone.

"Fuck," Jeff exclaimed, getting off the tile puller and looking toward the steps that led down to the tunnels.

Moments later, in a corridor, Phil pulled Mike to a stop.

Strangely agitated and not doing a good job hiding that he was very stoned, Phil spoke hurriedly. "I've thought about this a lot, Mike. We gotta talk to Gordon. Together. Gotta do it. Gotta."

Removing his mask, Mike seemed unsure. "Talk about what?"

"About him taking some time off, like ASAP. Now. Today. Let us do this," Phil replied as if he was saying the most obvious answer.

"What are you talking about?"

Mike could see where this was going but didn't want to enable Phil's opinion.

"He's become a liability, Mike."

Phil's face was serious, despite his glassy eyes.

For a long beat, Mike assessed Phil's demeanor before leaning in and sniffing. He could smell the marijuana from where he stood but felt he needed to make more of a show of it for Phil.

"I can see why you could be a little too paranoid... Know what I'm saying?" Mike said, shaking his head. "So, stop with the stupidity."

Ignoring him, Phil just got more intense. "Mike. He hit Wendy! Hit her. Told me he punched her in the nose."

Mike flinched, staring back, considering this revelation.

Phil let it sink in.

"Holy fuck" was all Mike could answer. "That can't be right."

Phil nodded gravely. "I got Craig starting tomorrow—and if word gets out about Gordo and Bill Griggs hears any of it? We are majorly fucked. You get that? If we lose this gig... we lose the bonus. You wanna take that chance?"

Inside a containment area on the next floor, Gordon, with his mask on, stared with an eerie calm at the poly sheet wall in front of him. Upon it, new graffiti had been sprayed. Two words. Words that made Gordon remove his mask and stare blankly at it.

All demons.

When was that done? he thought to himself.

Following the extension cable down the stairs, Jeff walked by the fence that separated the patients from the staff side and carried on toward the equipment annex.

He came to a stop at the base of the steps and looked ahead. With his flashlight already on, he gritted his teeth as the light around him faded to a weak dim. It was a murky light. Too murky to be called light. Even his flashlight did little to help.

Quickly stooping over, Jeff picked up the orange power cord in one hand, then followed it into the tunnel toward the breaker.

Phil was still standing in the hallway, lecturing Mike, who just stared back at him in unsure confusion.

"Even best-case scenario," Phil said, "work'll get done. But no doubt Craig will see Gordo's not on his game. And knowing Craig, he will spread it around. Our rep will be toast in the town. Meaning we probably won't get more jobs. So, we gotta get him to go *before* tomorrow, or he'll drag us—"

"What are you guys talking about?"

A voice came from a doorway.

Spinning in shock, neither Phil nor Mike had heard Gordon approach them, his limp almost dragging his leg along the floor.

Walking up, he stopped and looked between the two men, staring at both for a few seconds each before speaking. "Well? What were you saying?"

"About your nephew," Mike said, fumbling for an excuse.

To him, Gordon had grown more haggard since they started this job, and his instinct told him to be very cautious with his words. He didn't want to burn bridges just yet.

"Just sayin' about how the kid's coming along." Phil

slapped on a convincing smile—being a much better actor than Mike was.

"And how do you think he's coming along?" Gordon asked, frowning with suspicion.

Holding onto the orange cable like a lifeline, Jeff walked into the dark annex room, his torch held out straight ahead. Hurriedly, he noticed the breaker box, with the orange plug lying on the floor in front of it. Without stopping for a moment, he plugged the cord in, then turned and bolted back out.

Quickly making it to the daylight at the base of the steps, Jeff smiled with relief, hearing the music turn on upstairs, and the tile puller grumble back to life.

Relieved, he couldn't help but let out a big sigh.

He slowly began to walk up the stairs. Each step feeling more of a relief. Even though he didn't like what the dark did to him, sometimes, he had no choice but to suck it up. He turned the first corner.

Jeff gasped as he came to a sudden stop. He stared at a figure sitting on a step on the other side of the fence. The wire grating between them distorted his view.

A note of familiarity made Jeff squint and move in closer to see the figure more clearly.

"Holy shit," he exclaimed, recognizing the figure's hat and sunglasses. "Hank? Dude!"

But Hank did not move. He just sat, as if in a trance, slowly rocking.

"Dude?" Jeff asked again, trying to focus through the dark on the other side of the fence.

No response.

With a frown, he moved in closer and heard a quiet, muffled song pouring from Hank's headphones.

Jeff's frown turned into a smirk.

"Lost in music, huh?" Jeff said, leaning closer to the fence. "Yo, dude! HELLOOOO!"

Still no response.

"Hank?"

Moments passed of nothing.

Then, sluggishly, Hank turned to face him.

"You are in some deep shit y'know?" Jeff laughed.

"What are you doing here?" Hank slurred.

"What am *I* doing here?!" Jeff's laughter continued. "What the fuck are *you* doing here?! Everyone thinks you're in Miami at that school! Gordo and Phil want your head, man. Jeez."

"What are you... doing here?" Hank slurred again.

"Dude, did you score on a scratch or—" Jeff noticed Hank's hand, from which a viscous dark-red liquid dripped.

"What are you doing here..."

"L-Listen, man. I'm..." Jeff backed away, clearly freaked out. "I'm going to go get someone. Um... I'll be right back. You stay there, okay?"

Hank lifted his bloodied hand and opened his palm. In it lay a red-stained silver dollar. "What are you doing here?"

In the hallway above, Mike and Phil were still trying to allay Gordon's suspicions with their makeshift cover story.

"He's learning fast," Mike continued with a trembling voice. "He just needs a little motivation sometimes."

"Well, I promised my brother I'd hire him." Gordon's words were tinged with a stern suspicion. He then turned to Phil. "What do you think? About Jeff? My nephew?"

Phil, still smiling, shot a look to Mike, then back at Gordon. "A little slow, I guess. But now that Hank's gone, Craig'll be able to take up any slack from all this. Which brings me to—"

"Don't worry. I'll motivate him," Mike said.

Gordon smiled, and for a second, the tension dissipated, at least on face level. Taking the cellphone out of his pocket, he handed it to Mike. "It's almost noon, Mike. Call in lunch."

Without taking the cell, Mike shook his head. "I believe it's Phil's turn..."

"So wrong, my friend," Phil replied.

"Want me to go check the chart?" Mike countered. "I looked at it this morning. Without Hank, it comes round to you again."

"Fuck it," Phil said, rooting inside his pocket, then pulling out an old silver coin. "Let's just flip for it, shall we?"

"Whoa," Mike said, seeing the coin. "Where'd you

get that?"

"Just found it round here." Phil shrugged. "Pretty wild, huh?"

Gordon stared at the coin curiously.

"So, heads or tails?" Phil smiled, poising the coin, ready to flick.

"Instead of me proving you wrong, you'd rather do this?" Mike shook his head with a laugh. "Sorry about this, boss," he said to Gordon.

Phil just grinned back. "Which is it?"

"Heads."

Gordon continued staring at the coin silently.

As the coin was launched into the air—

On the stairs leading down to the tunnel, Hank's fist opened, dropping the bloodied coin onto the step below.

Phil caught the coin midair and slapped it onto the back of his hand. Uncovering it, he showed tails.

Phil smiled. "Loser, it is—"

Mike, on autopilot, took the phone from Gordon's hand. "Fine," he sighed. "I'll call it in."

Gordon, not noticing Mike take the phone, was too enamored with the coin. Reaching out, he took it from Phil's hand and held it up to examine it. He stared at the small metal disc in confusion, then at Phil, then back at the coin. "Something," he grumbled. "Some... thing. I know... I..."

"What?" Phil asked.

"HEY! HEY! YO!"

The call came from down the hallway.

They all turned in unison and saw Jeff running up to them.

"I found Hank!" Jeff exclaimed excitedly, out of breath. He lurched to a stop.

Phil and Mike stared at Jeff as if he had lost his mind.

"What are you talking about, Jeff?" Gordon asked with a frown.

"I just saw Hank," Jeff reiterated, pointing behind him. "I saw him on the steps to the breaker. He was just... sitting there. Sounded drunk to me."

Mike looked at Phil, then Gordon, with a bemused expression.

"I swear to God, guys! I *saw* Hank, I *saw* him."

Suddenly highly agitated, Phil took two steps over to Jeff and clipped him on the side of the head. "Don't be a fuckin' idiot, ya mullethead!"

"Fuck," Jeff shouted, stepping back. "I swear. Why the hell would I make that shit up, huh?"

"Why would Hank be here if he's in fuckin' Miami, *huh?*" Phil asked.

"How do I fuckin' know! But he's back there!"

Phil shook his head and waved dismissively. "Just get back to work! We'll bring you your lunch!"

"Where did you say he was, Jeff?" Gordon asked, ignoring Phil.

Phil turned to him, stunned. "You believe this punk? Don't care if he's your nephew. That's just bullshit."

"The staircase to the equipment room," Jeff replied. "I wouldn't make this up, Gordon."

"This is so stupid!" Phil spat. "So fucking stupid!"

Moments later, Jeff led Gordon across the gym, closely followed by Mike and Phil.

"This is ridiculous." Phil carried on complaining. "The dickhead's in Miami! Why would he be here? Why?! Amy told us where he was."

With cold determination, Jeff carried on, not answering Phil. Not giving his denials any more oxygen.

Jeff pointed to the staircase ahead. "Right down here," he said as they walked down the first flight. "He's right 'round—"

As they rounded the corner, Jeff stopped in disbelief. He pointed to the vacant spot on the step where he had seen Hank. "*There*, he was right there. On the step."

"God, this is stupid!" Phil shook his head. "We can't waste more time with this bull."

"I'm getting a bit hungry," Mike said as his stomach growled. "Can we just go eat now? He ain't here."

"I saw him!" Jeff protested. "Why would I say I saw him if I didn't see him!?"

Gordon, his face still stony, walked up to the top of

the steps and peered through the fence from a higher vantage point, looking straight down. Blinking, he spotted the red-stained coin lying in the dirt—just where Hank had dropped it.

"Jeff, I talked to Amy. *You* heard it," Phil said, trying to have a more reasonable tone. "Hank told her he won on a scratch and took off for Miami. You were there. *You heard it*. We *all* heard it!"

"No. We didn't," Gordon replied in a monotone.

The men all looked up at Gordon, who peered back down at them, a menacing look in his eyes.

Mike took a step up, wanting to escape the conversation. "I'm going to get lunch—" He moaned.

"*Stay right there*, Mike," Gordon barked, turning his attention back to Phil. "You told us that's what she said, Phil. We didn't *hear* her say it. We didn't *hear* a thing. Apart from you telling us that's what happened."

"What?" Phil replied in a squeak.

Gordon grimaced. "We *saw* you on the phone. We heard *you* talk. We didn't hear Amy say a thing."

"What?" Phil blurted, affronted, glancing to the others. "What are you sayin'? That I wasn't talking to Amy? I'm a liar now, am I?" He put a hand on Mike's shoulder. "Mike? C'mon, you know me."

Jeff stood by quietly, shocked at the argument he had caused.

"Give me back my cell, Mike," Gordon said, raining his voice, holding his hand out. "Now, give it."

"Why?" Phil asked. "He's gotta get lunch."

Gordon stared at Phil and spoke slowly and firmly, keeping the same tone. "I. Want. To. Call. Amy."

"What?! Why?! She told us what happened."

Phil's argument was getting seemingly more threadbare by the second.

"Gordon," Mike began, attempting to quell this surreal rising tension.

"Give me the cell, Mike."

"NO!" Phil shouted. "Mike, don't play into this madness! He's fuckin' losing it!"

Gordon started angrily down the stairs toward Mike.

"Hey, Gordon, relax," Mike pleaded in confusion as Gordon quickly squared up to him.

Staring close at Mike's face, the step giving him the height advantage he would never normally have, Gordon almost growled, "Give it to me!"

"See, Mike?" Phil exclaimed. "Just like I said, he beat his wife, and now he's fucking lost it!"

"SHUT THE FUCK UP, YOU JUNKIE," Gordon screamed at Phil before turning on Mike, bellowing furiously. "NOW, GIVE ME THE FUCKING PHONE!"

In a panic, Mike snatched the phone from his pocket and held it out to Gordon.

Phil stood, stunned at the outburst, not to mention the insult.

A sudden *THUNK, THUNK, THUNK, THUNK* above them cut the atmosphere almost in half. As all their eyes darted upward, the sound of heavy running footsteps traversed across the floor over them, sending clumps of dust falling from the ceiling.

The men stood in a short silence as the footsteps ran farther down a hallway leading off from the gym.

Jeff sighed with relief. "See? Hank *is* here! He's gotta be fuckin' with us."

Phil's eyes narrowed with confusion as the footsteps quietened to nothing.

Phil gritted his teeth. "Motherfucker." He grunted.

"What did I tell you?" Jeff beamed.

Gordon grabbed his cellphone from Mike. "You and Jeff go back that way to the tunnels in case he goes down the other stairs and turns back." He then glared at Phil. "And you? *You* come with me."

Phil didn't wait around to follow orders and just walked downstairs. "Fuck you, Gordon," he said loudly and clearly.

"Fine," Gordon looked at Jeff. "You go with Phil down there. Mike, we'll go up."

Mike sighed. "Whatever, boss."

He did not want any part of this, but didn't want to rile Gordon more.

Before Jeff could protest, Gordon and Mike quickly headed up the steps to the gym.

Mike trailed after a determined Gordon, annoyed to be wasting his time on what he thought was a wild goose chase. He just wanted lunch. He just wanted Phil and Gordon to go back to normal.

"It could be anyone walking around, Gordon," he implored. "Kids, some squatters, or someone?"

But Gordon ignored him and just strode down the corridor with determination.

Jeff stood at the bottom of the steps, looking down the dark tunnels.

"Let's just go back up?" he pleaded to Phil. "They'll have caught up to him by now."

"The tunnels are quicker," Phil said blindly, walking down to the right.

Jeff watched nervously, grabbing the small flashlight from his belt.

Mike and Gordon arrived at the first Ward C staircase, and as Gordon began to ascend, Mike stopped and listened.

Gordon noticed and turned. "What are you doing?" he asked, agitated at the sudden pause.

"You hear that?" Mike said, pointing down the steps. "Think we should go down."

They paused as Gordon listened.

"Probably Phil and Jeff," Gordon said.

"I swear I heard something else." Without waiting, Mike strode down the staircase.

"Mike?"

"You carry on up," Mike called back. "We'll find him."

"No!" Gordon shouted. "We stay together."

"We can cover more ground."

Mike's voice disappeared the farther down he went.

"Mike!"

But he was gone.

Annoyed, Gordon reluctantly turned up the staircase and continued limping upward.

Down on the tunnel level of the Ward C staircase, Mike peered back up the steps, making sure Gordon was totally out of sight.

"Fuck this shit," he mumbled. "They can fight this out on their own. I got better things to do." Grabbing his flashlight, he continued down the tunnels—heading for the staff library, in the opposite direction to Phil and Jeff.

Phil strode down the Ward A tunnel as if on a personal jihad.

Low wattage bulbs sailed by overhead, barely breaking through the darkness.

"Man, slow down," Jeff called out from behind, struggling to keep up.

As they passed a ladder pit leading into the lower steam tunnel system, Phil lurched to a stop. Peering down into the round entrance, he listened intently.

Quickly catching up, Jeff looked at the ladder as a cold sweat broke across his forehead. "I-I don't think he went down there. I can't hear anything."

But Phil obviously did—or thought he did.

Grabbing Jeff's flashlight and without a second's pause, Phil hurriedly climbed down the ladder into the dark steam tunnels.

"What are you doing?" Jeff cried out. "Why the hell would he be down there?! That's fuckin' stupid, man! Come back! Give me my light!"

In the library, Mike had jammed the wooden door shut by placing boxes of records against it, with no intention of partaking in his crew mates' paranoia and anger.

So, what if Hank was here? he mused. *He was no longer on the crew. A replacement was already called. What was Gordon gonna do? Kill him? For ditching work?*

On the countertop, Mike removed the last session tape from the box of Mary Hobbes's records.

Sliding the reel out, he read its label: *Session 9.*

167

Chapter 8

The Last Session

Phil stood at the bottom of the ladder pit, shining the flashlight up the rungs and into Jeff's nervous face peering back down.

"We should go upstairs," Jeff said.

Phil quirked a cocksure smile. "Just stay put. You don't need to go anywhere. Just call me on your walkie if you see or hear anything, okay?"

"But... I-I left my walkie in the van."

Phil rolled his eyes. "Just stay here." He sighed.

"Hey, Phil," Jeff shouted. "There's something I didn't tell you."

Phil looked back up to him.

Jeff continued. "I think he, Hank... had blood on his hands."

Without even considering what was said, Phil turned and walked deeper into the pitch-black steam tunnels.

Alone in the murky asbestos-filled tunnel, with only

the scant, dull bulbs to light the area, Jeff shrank back against the wall.

Nervously, he grabbed the respirator mask from his belt and pulled it over his face. Tightening the mask's straps, he looked around in a panic, expecting the worst to happen.

Gordon passed by the big painted B on the wall, then entered the second-floor hallway. A place in this hospital he had never been before.

Ahead, he noticed a dead raccoon in the middle of the floor, still smoldering with maggots.

He grimaced at the sight.

"Do you understand that Princess, Simon, and you are all inside of Mary? You understand this, right, Billy? You are all parts of Mary?" the doctor said, in as light a tone as he could muster.

"Yes sir, I know that," Billy replied with a broken voice, having just been sobbing.

"And if Mary is sick, then you are sick, too? All of you? Princess, too?"

"Yes," Billy replied.

The doctor paused, not wanting to push Mary's alter too far. *"And you* want *Mary to get better, right? So, Princess can get better, too, right?"*

Mike stared at the spinning reels, more engrossed than ever. A bead of sweat dripped down his forehead.

"*Y-Yes,*" Billy replied.

"*So, help her, Billy. Help me. Tell me! Tell me about that day, Billy. That day in Lowell.*"

A long silence. A long uncomfortable silence.

Mike looked at the fast-forward button, itching to press it to speed this up. He was obsessed enough but knew that it was only a matter of time before he had to get back to work, with Gordon and Phil having made up.

He really—

"*D-Danny was... was naughty,*" Billy said softly.

Jeff grew more impatient and nervous by the second. He looked one way, then the other, then down into the ladder pit.

"Ph-Phil?" he called down weakly.

Nothing.

"You there?" he asked louder.

Still nothing.

Around the tunnel, the utility lights flickered suddenly, making him shudder and glance everywhere, spooked.

Outside in the parking lot, the genny sputtered as it started to run out of gas.

Down in the medieval catacombs of the hospital's steam tunnels, mold and moisture coated everything.

The beam of Phil's light punched through the soupy haze like a lightsaber, pushing forward, strangely fearless in this grotesque environment.

Slowing in his tracks, Phil's ear pricked up. He closed his eyes to concentrate on what it was and where it could have been coming from.

Music?

Distant but clear enough to tell that it came from down the tunnel ahead.

Gordon walked the dark corridor of Ward B, making sure to avoid the raccoon. Passing it, he winced as the stench of the animal's demise hit his nostrils.

Poor guy must've got trapped, he thought to himself.

Ahead, light from the ward's small room striped the floorboards in a pattern. He silently walked through, peering into the rooms.

Hoping for no surprises.

The lighting in the tunnel pulsed as the generator ran drier.

Jeff gasped, staring down the ladder pit. But only saw darkness. "Fuck," he muttered in panic. "Fuck, fuck, fuck, fuck." He walked backward a few paces before turning and dashing to escape as light throbbed from bulbs draining of power.

"NO! I WON'T TELL! I won't scare her!" Billy shouted.

Mike wiped the growing sweat from his forehead, feeling the temperature in the small room rising. Uncomfortably so.

"She's a good girl! She doesn't need to know!"

Billy's voice echoed from the machine's tinny speaker. The louder he got, the more piercing the sound became, clipping when it got too loud.

"Mary doesn't need to know what, exactly?"

The doctor's voice was calm despite Billy's rising upset.

"She doesn't need to know what Simon did!" Billy shouted.

"Did to who, Billy?"

"To—to—to." Billy's voice fell quiet. *"To Danny!"*

"What did Simon do to Danny! Bil—"

Impatiently, Mike pressed the fast-forward button. He wanted so badly to hear this last tape but wanted to also leave.

The tape spewed the same back-and-forth. The doctor asking. Billy saying no.

With the tape sped up, words squealed by for a few seconds until he released the button.

"Me, Billy, Danny? Please tell me—"

He hit the fast-forward again for a few seconds.

"Help Mary, right?" the doctor resumed.

"I won't do it! Please, sir—"

Mike fast-forwarded again.

"Awful, it's just too awful," Billy screamed.

The music was louder and closer to him.

Reaching down, Phil picked up a brick from a pile. He clenched the stone and turned a corner.

The music grew even louder.

Around another corner, Phil's flashlight beam quickly dropped as the sound culminated in front of him.

In the glare of the light, Hank's Walkman and headphones were left in the dirt, still blaring his music.

Gordon, reaching one end of the corridor, heard a thud behind him. Turning back, he saw a shadowy figure burst out of a seclusion room at the other end and disappear around a corner.

"Dammit!" Gordon cried. "Hank! Get back here!"

As fast as he could manage, Gordon hurriedly limped back down the corridor after the figure.

Jeff, still in the tunnel, tried to find his way out. Tried to find where the staircase was.

Must have made a wrong turn, he nervously thought. *Fuck.*

As the generator outside struggled to continue to run, the lights along the tunnels spasmed. On. Off. On. Off. On. Off they went.

Walking farther down the steam tunnel, Phil's beam caught sight of something else on the floor that belonged to Hank.

His belt.

Then, a few paces later, his hat.

"What the—" Phil hissed, picking up his pace, sensing Hank had to be near.

Mike, still fast-forwarding the tape in fragments, tried desperately to hear an answer to a question he didn't fully know yet.

"Please wake him up—"

Fast-forward.

"NO. NO PLEASE—"

Fast-forward.

"You have to, Billy. Please, just—"

Fast-forward. Stop.

The bulbs in the tunnel went dark in a chain reaction as the last of the power shut down.

Bit by bit, section by section, the bulbs switched to black.

Jeff stood helplessly and whimpered as utility lights down the far end of the tunnel went black, then the next, then the next.

Getting closer and closer by the second.

"NO!" Billy screamed.

"WAKE HIM UP, BILLY," the doctor shouted, losing his temper to match Billy's volume.

A tidal wave of darkness rocketed toward Jeff as sections of light switched off.

Ripping off his mask, he turned and ran in the opposite direction, bouncing into the walls in a panic, asbestos chunks flying. Hoping to outrun the creeping dark. But the darkness was faster than his legs, and it soon enveloped him, and Jeff was thrown into total darkness.

Jeff screamed.

Groaning with irritation, Mike switched on his flashlight. The reel-to-reel opposite him lay dormant. Devoid of all power.

After hearing a crash, Gordon limped around a corner of Ward B and came face-to-face with a toppled gurney that blocked his path, the wheels on it still spinning.

Pushing it out of the way, he grimaced, then barreled toward a set of wooden doors, ignoring the pain in his thighs that pulsed like razors cutting into all of his nerves. His determination, though, was very strong.

"God, no," Jeff screamed in the dark, scrambling to find his way out.

Almost hyperventilating, he frantically ran his hands along the wall to claw his path forward, desperate to find any escape.

Ahead in the steam tunnels, as Phil moved on at a determined pace, he quickly caught sight of something in the shadows.

Mike walked to the top of the stairs. Putting his flashlight away, he crossed the bright gym and followed the trail of the main power cord that led to the kitchen, then outside to the parking lot, ultimately to the generator.

Gordon burst through the wooden doors to steps that led upward, where a big red A was painted on the wall.

A sinking feeling crept over him. A helpless, sickly feeling.

The same one he felt when he first came to this floor with Bill Griggs.

A noise from farther up the steps pulled Gordon's thoughts into clearer focus, to the pursuit.

Phil dashed through, then halted. There, ahead of him, coming into the view of his flashlight was Hank. Crouched on the stone floor. Half naked. Trembling. Still wearing his sunglasses.

Craning his neck up to Phil, he shivered, terrified and delirious. "What are you doing here?"

Phil stared blankly. All emotion lost on him from the shock. He squeezed the brick.

"Female Ward A, third floor," Gordon shouted over Phil's walkie-talkie, breaking the tension. "I-I found him."

Phil's face contorted in confusion, glancing down at the walkie, then back up to the trembling Hank.

At the far end of the tunnels, there were no sounds aside from those of Jeff screaming in panic.

Running.

Freaking out.

Trying to find a way out.

Gordon cautiously walked up the steps of stairwell A to the third floor.

At the top of the flight, beyond a closed door off the ward corridor—wheezing and sounding terrified—a half-naked figure hid in the shadows.

Skeletal and trembling, with crazed, wild eyes, it suddenly bolted across the darkness and through a doorway on the other side.

Reaching the top of the steps, Gordon stood next to the words *Extreme Ward. Escape Precautions* painted in black capitals onto the gray, damp wall.

Turning to his right, he stared down the length of the same taped-off, murky corridor from before.

Eerie light spilled from the last seclusion, illuminating the restraint chair in the middle of the corridor.

Just as everyone else, Gordon's flashlight did little here. Nothing but display more rot and decay.

His breath sounded more labored as a chill crawled over him.

"Gordon, come back."

Phil's voice came through loud and shrill on his walkie-talkie.

With a sigh of relief that he was not alone, Gordon picked up the walkie. "Yeah, Phil?"

"Where are you?"

"I told you, Ward A, third floor. Hank's up here."

"Okay." Phil sounded annoyed. "I'm coming to you. Stay there. We gotta talk."

Out in the parking lot, Mike finished gassing the genny with one of the last fuel cans. He pulled on the genny's cord.

Once.

Twice.

On the third, the genny shrieked to life, as if rising from the dead with a scream.

In the library, the electricity flooded through the cables.

The light snapped on.

The reel-to-reel warbled to life.

"Please, Billy," the doctor said, exhausted, about to give up.

The hiss from the tape seemed to get louder with each second, filling the room with a claustrophobic static.

Until, as if from the depths of a deep well, a voice spoke. A guttural, terrifying voice.

"Hello, Doc."

Lights sprang to life along the whole length of the tunnel, section by section. In a section under the Male wing.

Swallowed in fiber and dust, Jeff pressed himself flat against a wall. Terrified as the lights above him burst on.

With his mask slung around his neck, he was white, literally. Coated head to foot in a fine dust. Asbestos.

"Are you Simon?" the doctor asked with a note of caution in his voice.

"You know who I am," Simon said gleefully, sadistically.

It sounded as if hell itself had a voice. All within the small body of Mary Hobbes.

Jeff looked at his dusted hands and body and screamed in panic.

At the entrance of Ward A's third-floor corridor, Gordon mustered all his strength, then ducked under the caution tape.

As he walked painfully down the ward, his limp was worse, his pain increasing.

"Billy has told me a lot about you," the doctor said.

"Billy is a smart boy," Simon replied over a lascivious chuckle.

Passing some of the seclusion rooms, the rotting floorboards creaked and moaned dangerously below Gordon's heavy footsteps.

Without checking any of the other rooms, he walked

toward the far end, to the last seclusion room next to the restraint chair.

Something... something was telling him to go there.

Down in the steam tunnels, Phil walked back through the dim passage with a fierce determination.

In the library, the reel spun in the empty room. Playing the session to no one.

"Simon, what happened in Lowell?" the doctor asked.

"Why don't you let Billy tell you?"

Every word Simon spoke sounded like a perversion, one he got a thrill out of.

"He was afraid it would scare Princess."

"Who the fuck is Princess?" Simon asked with a sudden flair of annoyance.

"A friend of Mary's," the doctor explained. *"Like you."*

"I never met her, Doc. And trust me, no one is like me."

On a cracked floorboard ahead of Gordon, something glinted in his flashlight beam, a coin. A very old coin.

Reaching down with a wheeze, Gordon picked it up.

"Tell me what happened to Danny."

Simon laughed. "Oh, use your imagination."

Recalling Phil had flipped a similar coin, Gordon blinked rapidly.

Wanting to see a correlation. Wanting to figure out what was happening. Wanting to... sleep.

His exhaustion was getting to be too much.

His pain was getting to be too much.

He stared at the coin, trying to piece the puzzle together. Convinced the answer was right in front of him.

He did not even notice the chuckle in the back of his mind. The deep, guttural chuckle. The chuckle that sounded far yet near.

Blinking faster, he carried on walking, staring at the coin.

"I'd rather you tell me, Simon," the doctor implored. *"Billy got very upset when I asked. It's not fair on him."*

Getting closer to the last seclusion room, Gordon's feet walked by a growing trail of old coins. Like bread crumbs, they were scattered, leading the way straight into the space.

On the second floor of Ward B, Phil walked by the toppled gurney, his expression unreadable, fists clenched.

"Danny was naughty, Doc," Simon said with satisfaction.

The illuminated restraint chair was covered in a billowing of black mold. The dark fungus growing over every part of the once-white leather straps.

"What did Danny do?" the doctor asked as a fear crept into his voice.

Phil passed the big painted A on the staircase wall, then began his ascent and reached into his pocket and pulled something out.

"He shouldn't have done it," Simon chuckled.

Mike walked in through the kitchen from outside, then across the broken tiles toward the gym.

High above him, from a balcony at the top of the

room, a figure stared intently down at him. As clear as day.

At the threshold to the last seclusion, Gordon paused, squinting in the sunlight that poured in through the unblocked window inside. A white brilliance almost blinding from the dark his eyes had adapted to.

"He broke Mary's doll, Doc." Simon sighed. *"He pulled off her head."*

Gordon looked down at his feet and saw more coins, hundreds of them from across many years. These along with wristwatches, spectacles, brooches, and earrings. And next to them, a leather satchel. Hank's leather satchel.

Recognizing it, Gordon's mind spun. He trembled, peering into the seclusion.

Pink paint peeled from the walls inside. Each of them plastered with faded old images of dolls, Christmas trees, Santa...

"It wasn't such a nice thing to do, Doc. Was it?"

Gordon limped in with a stagger and peered at the faded nameplate on the door: *Hobbes, M.*

Farther down the hall, Phil ducked under the yellow caution tape, shining his flashlight over the damp decay of the Ward A corridor.

"Gordo?" he called out with trepidation.

"So, I..." Simon said with a laugh. "I..." He paused, stifling his laughter, and his tone turned grave and blunt. "*I pulled off Danny's head, Doc. Well, cut his throat anyway—good thing his knife was brand new. I would like to have finished the job, though. He would have looked much better if I took it clean off. But we all miss opportunities, don't we?*"

In Phil's free hand, he had pulled out his box knife, holding it as a weapon. He peered in all the rooms he passed, waiting to find Gordon in one of them.

"*It was a brand-new knife and was real, real sharp.*" Simon cackled again.

Gordon stopped inches from the pink wall in the seclusion.

His eyes widened with confusion and terror.

He reached out and touched a single photo stuck to the wall.

A new photo.

A photo of his daughter.

Emma.

Pasted onto the wall with red slime.

Gordon's expression twisted.

The photo. *That same photo* was also in his wallet.

He thought for a second, then quickly pulled out his wallet. Searching its folds, he noticed that his photo of Emma was missing. Staring at the photo, he thought back to Monday, when Phil took his wallet to pay for lunch.

Carefully, Gordon peeled the picture of his daughter from off the wall.

Suddenly, his attention was pulled to other photos decorating the cracked plaster.

Ones of Wendy. Of him. Of Emma. Of Phil.

"Oh, there was a lot of blood. So much blood, Doc." Simon spoke with pride. *"But I know Mary wanted me to do it. I felt her need. I felt her hate. I felt her sadness."*

Overwhelmed, Gordon sank to his knees as the photo of Emma slipped through his fingers and fell to the floor.

"Of course, I wanted to do it, too, Doc."

Phil walked by the moldy restraint chair, then glanced into Mary Hobbes's seclusion room.

He peered in at Gordon, who was on his knees in front of a wall, looking up at the photos. Even from his vantage point, Phil could see the sinister tableau made up of dozens of pictures from Emma's christening. Photos of guests, of smiles, of love. And Gordon, kneeling, crying.

Jeff burst out the kitchen's side exit and into the bright sunlight of the hospital's garden, sputtering, clawing at his clothes, as if a thousand bees were attacking him.

Falling onto the grass, he rolled around, yelping hysterically, desperate to get rid of the white poisoned powder.

"Gordon?" Phil said from the threshold of the seclusion room. "What is this?"

Gordon slowly turned and saw Phil looking back, box knife in hand.

As he went to speak, Gordon's mind spun a one-eighty. He felt dizziness uproot his center of gravity. The vision of Phil whirled as his judgmental stare then shone a brilliant yet terrifying yellow.

"Help me," Gordon managed to plead, feeling his own exhaustion rip through him.

Still in the gym, Mike stood, staring up at the balcony. Having seen the shadowy figure peering down from above.

Not at all afraid, he just looked up, fascinated.

The figure raised a bony finger at him.

"What do you mean" was all that he could say. Unsure of how to react, Mike then heard a footstep behind him.

Jeff frantically opened the van door, manically brushing the asbestos powder from his face and hair. He stifled his breathing as best he could, conscious not to inhale any more of the fiber.

Gritting his teeth, he forced himself to pause. He had to stop. He had to focus. He had to calm down.

Quickly getting into the passenger seat, he grabbed his walkie-talkie from the dashboard. "G-Gordon? Ph-Phil?" he spluttered weakly into the walkie. "Please, someone come back. I think I am covered in that stuff. I need help."

Nothing came back.

"Gordon, Phil, Mike. Hank? Anyone? Please, come back. Please!" He gasped, drawing a sharp breath, feeling his breathing losing control through his panic. "I'm outside! By the vans! Please, someone help. I dunno what to do."

No response.

He gasped again and held the walkie to his chest, trying to catch his breath.

The walkie then sprang to life with garbled static.

"I'm coming. I'm coming," the voice said.

Jeff, in his panic, couldn't tell who spoke but smiled happily anyway. "Thank God," he cried, clicking off the walkie and tilting his head back on the seat rest.

His hand fell between the seats and brushed something sticking out from the back, a grocery bag with chocolates and a bunch of dying, wilted flowers still in their cellophane wrapping.

Chapter 9

Friday

Down in the staff library of the Danvers State Hospital, the session tape had finished, yet still spun the reels 'round and 'round, as a tail of the cassette slapped the machine.

TCHICK, TCHICK, TCHICK, TCHICK.

The open folder on the table lay unmoved, and the sinister photo of the shaven-headed Mary Hobbes stared out with her unhinged smile.

TCHICK, TCHICK, TCHICK, TCHICK.

In the parking lot, the crew's vehicles were sat just as they had left them the day before. The wind blew a collection of dead leaves across the cracked asphalt, creating an ominous, deserted atmosphere.

In the parking lot, behind the driver's seat of the van, Gordon sat. He looked awful, haunted, and, somehow, more exhausted. He stayed motionless, clutching his cell phone.

The walkie on his seat next to him sprang to life, with a heavy static.

"Come back," Phil said, his words heavily static and almost incomprehensible. "Come back. Gordon? It's Phil."

Gordon weakly picked up the walkie, slurring, "This is Gordon."

"We found the one," Phil said, the static crackles almost deafening but Phil's glee audible.

Gordon tried to think for a moment, tried to gather his thoughts.

How did he get here? He remembered being in the room. He remembered the photo of Emma. He remembered Phil carrying the box knife.

"We found the one responsible," Phil said. "I'm in the decon room."

Gordon's eyes widened.

After a beat, a tiny exhausted smile crept over his face. He opened the van door and got out, closing it behind him, not noticing the dried bloody handprint smeared onto the paintwork.

Still gripping his cell phone, Gordon entered kitchen side entrance and limped through the building. Crossing the large room, his leg buckled with each step.

Across the gym, he descended the stairs and journeyed within the tunnels slowly, wheezing as the pain seared through him.

His expression remained catatonic.

Traversing the tunnels, he ascended to Ward C, slowly but determined. Soon enough, he approached the decontamination room, where its plastic-lined walls puffed in and out with the wind.

Gordon stopped and peered inside. A shadowy, distorted figure stood within.

"In here, Gordon," Phil's familiar voice softly said.

The gates to the hospital opened, and a blue Corvette came speeding up the path before coming to a grinding halt next to Gordon's parked van.

The door to the car flipped open, and a man in his thirties hopped out. Craig McManus. Arriving for his first shift with Gordon's abatement crew.

Wearing a backward Red Sox cap and smoking a Lucky Strike, he carried with him an air of cockiness. One he had earned and deserved through being one of the best at his job in the state.

Leaning into his car, he removed a cloth bag containing all the kit he needed, overalls and tools. He was more than ready to start, and with a promised equal share of the bonus for only three days' work, he considered himself damn lucky.

Slamming the door shut, he looked up at the looming Kirkbride building. "Freakin' beautiful," he muttered with a smile. "Gonna be a pleasure working with ya, babe."

Through the hospital's front entrance, Craig wandered across its empty foyer and toward the north hallway.

As he looked around, he noticed how void of life everything was. Pausing for a moment, he listened, hoping to hear the sound of machinery or crew chatter. But there was nothing.

"Hello? Phil?" he called out, his voice echoing. "Gordon? Better not be fucking with me."

Passing a gurney, complete with restraint straps, he stared in fascination. "So cool."

He did not see the figure lurking in his periphery. Staring at him, clutching a metal pipe.

Gordon hobbled through the plastic sheets and into the decontamination room.

Immediately, he saw Hank laid out in the middle of the room, spread-eagle, with no clothes on, strangely still wearing his sunglasses. He was not moving.

Gordon covered his mouth in shock, feeling an urge to vomit. He took a few deep breaths in and stared up at Phil in horror. "What did you do?"

"He was a liability, boss," Phil replied, coming out from behind a sheet near the open window. His words were spoken gently and lightly, as if whispering to a newborn. "There was nothing we could do. You know that, right? It had to be done."

Gordon looked down at Hank, hand still over his

mouth. "Why? Why did you do this?" he spluttered, trying to keep his composure.

"He brought it on himself, Gordon." Phil's soft voice was so out of place it made every word spoken seem sinister. "He was in the wrong place at the wrong time, with the wrong body and the wrong mind." He smirked. "Typical Henry."

"Y-You did it," Gordon said. "You *killed* him. W-Why?"

Phil's expression dropped to a sneer. He slowly cocked his head. "Wake up!" He shouted in anger.

The words hit Gordon like a stone. He stepped back in shock.

"*Wake up*, Gordon! *Look* at him!" He pointed at Hank.

Gordon looked again.

"Look *real close!*" Phil added. "*CLOSER!*"

Gordon turned from Phil and crouched over the body. His thigh screaming at him.

Shaking his head, he didn't know what to look at. He slipped off Hank's sunglasses, hoping this was all a joke.

Gordon stared in horror at Hank's left eye, a swollen, pus-dripping blister with a metal lobotomy pick protruding from near his tear duct lodged deep in his skull.

Gordon blanched and gagged, feeling bile rising in his throat.

"W-What are you doing here?" Hank sloppily mumbled, still alive. Blankly staring at the ceiling.

Gordon scrambled back, appalled, terrified. A look of utter confusion in his eyes.

Struggling, Hank opened his mouth again, his lips cracking. "What are you doing here?"

Gordon rubbed his ear furiously and trembled.

He saw something in his mind. Something he couldn't place. A vision. A memory. Something he imagined—Hank, rounding a corner, carrying a satchel full of coins. Lurching to a stop, turning and looking guilty, riddled with panic.

"What are you doing here?" Hank had mumbled with a nervous smile.

Gordon couldn't stop blinking, trying to process the images in his head, as well as the scene in front of him. Ferociously rubbing his ear.

He blinked more and turned to look up at Phil, who was rubbing his ear the same way.

"Hank needs help," Gordon said feebly. "We need to call an ambulance."

Dropping his hand, Phil quickly shook his head. "Oh, you can't let anyone know about this. If they learn about him, they'll learn about the others, too."

Gordon slowly stood up straight, painfully moving up from the floor. His trembling increased. He then pointed at Phil. "You *did* this. *You*." He spat the words at Phil in a sudden fury. "Why? Did you poison me? Is that what's happening?"

Phil stared back. "Gordon, come on—"

"It all makes sense to me now," Gordon scoffed. "You

are setting me up!"

"You're asleep," Phil said.

Gordon pointed again at Phil. "Those kids. The ones I saw you with. The ones you lied about. At first, I thought you were getting your drugs." He laughed bitterly. "But I see it now. *You* hired those kids to *kill* Hank. He took your Amy, so you wanted revenge."

"Open your eyes," Phil said calmly.

Gordon gritted his teeth. "I've had enough. Now, where are the others?"

"*Wake... up. Wake... up.*"

"*Where are they?!*"

"Wake up, Gordon!"

"*I am fucking awake!*" Gordon screamed as spittle flew from his mouth.

"Uh... Hi?" a small voice meekly spoke from the doorway.

Phil ticked a crooked, sinister grin as Gordon slowly turned to see Craig awkwardly standing there with a quizzical smile.

"Sorry, but what's going on, Gordon? Are you guys fucking with me?"

Gordon just stared at Craig blankly.

Phil, meanwhile, chuckled and shook his head.

"What's so funny?" Gordon said.

Craig stepped in. "Hey, who are you talking to?"

Gordon frowned, struggling to figure something out. A storm raged inside his skull as he dug at his ear again.

He glanced down at Hank, then up to...

No one. No Phil.

Craig walked in the room and noticed Hank on the ground, confused. "This some sort of new-guy hazing. Very funny. I heard you guys were jokers!"

Gordon turned to Craig as his vision spun off its axis.

"Very funny. You got me," Craig said, stepping next to Gordon and looking down at Hank with a smile.

Craig saw the damage to Hank's eye, and his jaw dropped in horror.

Gordon, expression blank, dropped his phone. He lunged at Craig and grabbed him in a half nelson. Gordon spun him, then flung him to the cement with surreal strength, right next to Hank.

In a blur, Gordon clambered on top of Craig. With a free hand, he snatched the nub of the metal pick lodged in Hank's skull and pulled it out violently. Killing Hank almost in an instant.

Craig screamed to no avail as Gordon turned the bloody pick onto him and slammed it down into his open eye with ease.

Craig's legs jerked outward, and he gripped Gordon's arm. He saw Gordon's chillingly calm demeanor pressing against the pick, pushing it beyond his eye and farther into his head.

The poor man's arms sprang out, then flapped in a bizarre reflex, looking as if he was trying to fly away. But the hold on him was too tight to escape.

As Gordon straddled the man, he stared blankly at the wall ahead, not meeting Craig's eyeline once, and twisted the pick, mushing it through Craig's frontal cortex. Gordon, with his vacant expression and twisting hand, resembled a bored chef stirring soup.

Within a few terrible seconds, Craig's arms went abruptly slack, the pick having impaled a violent trail into his brains.

Gordon stopped moving as well and, for a few seconds, stayed in place.

He then rose off his body and wiped his bloody hands on his trousers.

He peered down at Hank's body and saw a vision—Hank lay on the dirt of the tunnel, screaming, as Gordon stood over him. Loot spilled across the ground beside him. Gordon grabbed the metal pick from the pile of coins. Before Hank could react, he jammed it into Hank's eye, immediately moving it left and right with sadistic glee. Lobotomizing Hank in the most terrible way.

Bending down next to Craig's and Hank's bodies, Gordon picked up his cell phone and limped out of the decontamination room in a daze.

Down the length of the ward, he shambled.

On the floorboards ahead, a swath of blood led into one of the seclusion rooms on the left. From inside, two feet stuck out of the doorway. Lifeless and limp.

Phil.

His body cold and twisted on the floor. His face had been lacerated so badly barely any skin remained on his skull.

Phil stared at Gordon, box knife in hand. "I found Hank," he said with repressed anger. "He's hurt bad. Talking gibberish. But he did manage to tell me that you did it to him. That you hurt him, Gordon."

Gordon turned and, with a lifeless expression, rushed at Phil. In an instant, Gordon had wrestled the box knife from Phil's hand, then turned it back on him.

Gordon passed the next seclusion room. The floorboards cracked and moaned under his limping weight.

Inside the room, a body in a hazmat suit lay face down, its head caved in, exposing a large crater.

Mike stood in the center of the gym, watching as Gordon strode toward him. "Genny died," he said with a smile, trying to gauge Gordon's vacant expression. "You find Hank?"

Before he could say any more, Gordon bashed in Mike's head with a lump hammer.

Crashing to the floor, Mike whimpered as Gordon hammered him over the head again and again and again.

Up on the balcony, the shadowy figure could only watch in silence.

In the last seclusion room, Jeff's lifeless body lay in a heap. His head severed and hanging back, almost decapitated, throat exposed like some kind of grotesque Pez dispenser, with a box knife jammed down the trachea.

Jeff, eating from the chocolate box he had found in the grocery bag, stepped out of the passenger door of the van.

He felt much better than he did back in the tunnels. Relieved that he got through to someone on the walkie-talkie, he made a pact to himself that this would be his last day working on this job.

Glancing up, he saw Gordon steamrolling out of the Kirkbride and toward him at a fast pace.

"I was freakin' out." Jeff smiled. "All the lights went out. It was crazy."

Jeff did not notice his uncle's face was smattered with blood until it was too late.

"Hey, I found these chocolates. Hope it's okay that I—"

Jeff did not see the box knife swing at his neck and sever his windpipe in a single savage action. Nor did he see Gordon maintain a monstrously empty expression, slicing and slicing and slicing even deeper into his neck.

At the end of the corridor, Gordon stopped his slow stumble and stood motionless for a few moments. Wavering slightly under his own weight. He barely focused on anything as his mouth hung slack.

Chapter 10

The Weak & The Wounded

T he night brought with it an unseasonable chill to Danvers. An icy wind from the Atlantic washed over the town, hitting the hospital with vigor.

In the building, the abatement crew had left various windows open, allowing this bitter breeze to fill every darkened corner of its decaying shell.

The generator in the cracked parking lot still ran, feeding power to the utility lights that fed throughout the hospital. Its hum was a soothing sound that joined the chorus of crickets in the nearby grass.

Up on the third floor of Ward A, in Mary Hobbes's seclusion room, the bright moonlight shone in through the window, illuminating Gordon, who sat cross-legged in front of the wall of photos.

He moved his hands over each one, of his wife. Of his baby. Of his lovely life.

From the floor, he picked up the wallet-sized photo of Emma he had dropped before. Then, dipping his hand in a puddle of red slime pooled next to him, he coated the back of it, then stuck it into place.

Breaking through this silence, his cell phone rang loudly.

Slowly, almost too slowly, he picked it up.

"Hello, baby," he said lovingly into the receiver. "Thanks for calling back. I know it's hard... No, please listen... Please, baby..." He began to sob. "I know. I know. I am so sorry. Can you forgive me?... I don't know... I don't know why I did it. Can you find it in your heart to forgive me?" He listened some more. "I will never ever do it again, baby... What? No, I promise... I just want to come home. I just want to be home with you and Emma." Gordon turned his head to glance out of the window, up at the moon. "I love you both so much. Please, baby, let me come home now..."

A beam of moonlight highlighted the cell's missing battery.

"I beg you. Can I please come home? Please..."

After a moment, he heard a milky, liquid voice reply.

"Yes, baby. You can come home now. I forgive you," Wendy said through the phone's speaker.

Gordon couldn't help but smile. "Oh, Wendy... Thank you, baby. I love you..."

"I love you, too, Gordon," the spectral voice replied. *"It's time for you to come home now. We miss you."*

Gordon wiped a grateful tear from his cheek.

He then blinked suddenly. Unexpectedly.

"I miss you... Love. I..." he said, suddenly dazed.

He then felt something on his face. Lifting his hand, he touched his brow, a warm liquid dripping down.

Turning in shock, he looked up behind him and saw a figure in the darkness holding a bloodied metal pipe.

———

PATIENT RELEASE ASSESSMENT
Date: April 4th, 1992
Patient: 92738-Benson, Deborah
Date of Birth: February 23rd, 1901
Date of Committal: October 16th, 1922
Reason for Committal: Parricide (9 members)

Patient Diagnosis: Borderline Personality Disorder (BPD), Obsessive Compulsive Disorder (OCD), Cognitive Decline, Schizophrenia, Paranoid Personality Disorder (PPD), Schizoaffective Disorder.

Release Assessment: Patient (81), has been a long-term resident of Danvers State Hospital. Over the course of her 70-year treatment, patient has exhibited numerous persistent psychiatric conditions above. Despite the severity and chronic nature of these conditions, patient has not displayed any violent tendencies since her initial committal. While there has been no significant improvement in her disorders, her advanced age and physical health status suggest a diminished capacity for aggression or self-harm. Given her life expectancy, the likelihood of her posing a threat to herself or others is considerably reduced.

Upon comprehensive evaluation, it is evident that the patient continues to suffer from severe psychiatric symptoms. Her BPD is characterized by emotional instability, intense interpersonal conflicts, and impulsive behaviors. Her OCD manifests as pervasive and intrusive thoughts, leading to repetitive and ritualistic behaviors that she is unable to control.

Cognitive decline is apparent, with marked memory impairment and decreased executive functioning. Her schizophrenia presents hallucinations, delusions, and disorganized thinking, significantly impairing her ability to function independently. The PPD exacerbates her distrust and suspicion of others, while the Schizoaffective Disorder contributes to mood disturbances and psychotic episodes.

Despite these ongoing issues, Ms. Benson's overall behavior has remained stable. The multidisciplinary team, including the board of psychiatrists, psychologists, and social workers, has determined that her risk of harm is minimal and the cost of further incarceration too great to justify.

Given the impending closure of Danvers State Hospital and the assessment that Ms. Benson does not pose a significant danger, it is recommended that she be released into a suitable community-based setting. Continuous monitoring and appropriate support will be necessary to manage her ongoing mental health needs.

Prepared by:
Doctor J. Gettler
Assistant Psychiatrist, DSJ
April 4th, 1992

———

Into the beam of moonlight spilling into Mary Hobbes's seclusion room, the figure stepped forward toward Gordon. Out of the shadows, so he could see them clearly.

With long matted hair, a twisted body, skin very old and wrinkled, this naked figure was evidently female but seemed more feral than human. Coated from head to foot in dirt and grime. She stared, wide-eyed, at Gordon.

"This is my home," she roared in fury, holding a bloody iron bar high above her head. Around her wrist, a tattered, dirty medical wristband read in faded letters, *92738-Benson, D. (Ward A).*

Gordon stared, momentarily confused. Holding the powerless phone in his hand, still on his call.

"Something's... wrong..." he mumbled.

"Tulips! They smell lovely. What's the occasion?" Wendy's voice said over the phone.

Smash!

Gordon wilted under the iron bar's second blow as his battery-less phone clattered to the floor.

"I know you, demon!" the old woman shouted. *"I recognize you. I saw you. I SEE YOU. You cannot take me, too!"*

Dazed, Gordon tried to lift himself off the ground.

Smash!

His head hit the floor boards with a bone-crunching *thunk* as blood sprayed from his ear.

Smash!

"I would recognize your filth anywhere!" the old woman shouted, then let out a defiant banshee wail.

Bloody sputum bubbled out of Gordon's nose as his eyes twitched, his body unable to move.

The woman staggered over and looked down at him. She quivered like a leaf, terrified in her rage, dropping the pipe.

"Demons are not welcome in my home," she muttered as she backed away, out of the seclusion room and into the darkness.

Gordon could only stare, unable to move, barely able to breathe or think.

He gazed at the powerless phone on the floor as blood seeped from his gaping wound.

"Not here, Gordon. Later." Wendy giggled on the phone. *"Oh, Gordon, I'm so happy for you. For us."*

208

Gordon's eyes widened. His life drained fast, but he could finally face clarity.

He began to remember.

From the phone's speaker, Gordon could hear boiling water bubbling, then the sudden clatter of a metal pot, followed by a crash. He then heard his own scream.

"Gordon!" he heard Wendy yell.

From the phone, the sound of an angry roar, followed by more terrified screams.

"No, Gordon! Please!" Wendy screamed. *"Stop it! No! Noooooo!"*

Gordon stared as his eyes welled with tears. The sound of the awful struggle bleeding from the phone speakers were deafening, seeping into his own mind.

Screams.

His dog barking.

Emma wailing.

Wendy gagging, spluttering.

His own heavy breathing.

A primal scream.

The dog growling defensively.

A thud.

The dog yelping and squealing.

Another thud.

Emma.

Emma crying.

Emma screeching.

Gordon stared in tearful horror. From the corner of

his eye, he could see his daughter's photo stuck to the wall, smiling at him innocently.

Her wailing continued to ring in his ears until he heard his own rageful roar, followed by her muffled cries. Tortured and gasping.

Then nothing.

Silence.

In the last ebbs of his life, Gordon could not even cry nor make a sound. He could only remember. Remember everything as his tears continued.

Then, on the phone, he suddenly heard a raspy breath. Guttural, monstrous, and very clear and very present. The last thing he would ever hear.

"You're welcome, Gordon," a deep voice gleefully whispered. *"We had fun, didn't we?"*

———

As the dawn arrived the next morning, the cold of the night had given way to the warmth of the day.

In the car park of the Danvers State Hospital, the generator's hum sputtered and died once again, plunging the hospital into an even deeper silence and darkness.

As the day wore on, the town of Danvers would remain oblivious to what had happened at the hospital. But in time, the truth would at least become partially revealed. The tale would become a footnote in the grim history of the building. Another of madness and despair to frighten the children. A dismal chapter that would be forgotten soon enough.

———

"So, if Billy lives in the eyes," the doctor said. *"And Princess lives in the knees, with Mary living in her soul... Where does that leave you, Simon? Where do you live?"*

Simon chuckled. *"Doc, I live in desperation... I live in hurt... I live in pain... I live..."*

His voice fell gravelly.

"I live in the weak and the wounded."

Epilogue

The freshly repainted walls of the darkened seclusion room loomed menacingly over the small, fragile body of Mary Hobbes. She lay, shackled, with leather restraints to the cold, metal-framed hospital bed.

Dressed in a pristine hospital gown, with her head freshly shaved, Mary's eyes darted back and forth under her closed eyelids. Tormented by nightmares that now plagued her unconsciousness.

The only illumination came from the open doorway at the other end of the room, and moonlight that weakly spilled in through the small, barred window, high up the wall above.

The shadows shrouded her, obscuring her features from Doctor David Adams and the burly orderly who looked in from the hallway. Their figures silhouetted by the dim light behind them.

"Why'd she get her own room, Doc?" the orderly asked, his voice a whisper.

"She's just a child," Doctor Adams replied as he peered down at the open chart in his hands. "Shouldn't be in a shared room yet. Not until she is older."

"*Just* a child?" The orderly chuckled darkly. "Right. I cleaned all the blood off her. There's nothing *just* about her."

"She hasn't spoken since she arrived. Is that correct?"

"Nah." The orderly shook his head. "I even tried talking to her as I hosed her off. But nothing. Nada. She's locked up tight."

"Questions?" the doctor asked pointedly. "And what questions would those be, *exactly*? You know you shouldn't converse with new arrivals until after assessment."

Shifting uncomfortably, the orderly smiled nervously, his bravado now crumbled under the doctor's gaze. "Nothing much, I swear... just asked how she was, that kinda stuff..." He smiled apologetically. "I know I shouldn't have talked, but she looked so... I dunno. Out of it. Like, there but not there. Like she saw me. Looked at me. Something was wrong... I felt bad for her..."

The doctor exhaled in disappointment.

"Don't matter anyhoo," the Orderly continued hastily. "She didn't say squat."

The doctor shook his head, then turned his attention back toward Mary in her room. "Well, she's sedated now. So, I should—"

"Can you help us, Doc?" A boy's voice burst out from within the shadows. Billy's voice. As his words left Mary's mouth, she lay on her bed, hidden in the shadows, still very much asleep.

"Shhh," the small childlike voice of Princess added. "We're not supposed to talk to them, Billy! Simon said so!"

"But they could help us!" Billy retorted.

"We have to shhh!" Princess repeated pleadingly. "D'you wanna wake him?"

Billy quickly fell silent.

Despite her alters speaking, Mary's eyes continued to move under her lids. In her nightmares, her mind replayed the horrific events of the past twenty-four hours. Plaguing her with visions that she could not comprehend. She was lost, totally disconnected from what was happening in her hospital room.

Over the next few moments, a thick, suffocating silence filled the seclusion. A silence where only Mary's labored breathing could be heard.

"Mary?" the doctor eventually asked, his bassy voice breaking through the eerie quiet. "What do you need help with?"

"How's she awake, Doc?" the orderly asked in a whisper, his voice tinged with fear. "She should have had enough to floor an elephant."

The doctor ignored the question. "My name is Doctor Adams," he spoke kindly. "I *can* help you if you tell me what you need. Are you hungry? Thirsty? Are your restraints too tight?"

Nothing.

"Mary?" he called out. "Please answer me—"

"When can we leave, Doc?" Billy replied, his voice now barely above a whisper.

"Leave?" the doctor echoed, his brow furrowing. "I don't think—"

"Mary wants to go home." Billy's voice sounded as if it were on the verge of tears. "I want to go home."

Doctor Adams swallowed as he considered a reply but, instead, motioned to the door. "Let us leave her until tomorrow's assessment. This is delirium."

With an unsure look, the orderly complied and shut the door, thrusting the room into near blackness. The moonlight doing very little.

Billy broke the silence once more with a whimper. "You gotta help us, Doc, or... or I dunno what's gonna happen." As his words trailed, he sobbed into silence.

"I know what will happen," a lascivious voice replied.

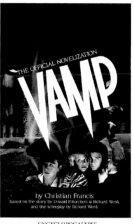

ENCYCLOPOCALYPSE
ISBN-13: 9781959205364
ISBN-10: 1959205366

ENCYCLOPOCALYPSE
ISBN-13: 9781960721068
ISBN-10: 1960721062

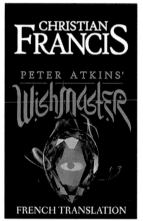

FAUTE DE FRAPPE
ISBN-13: 9782491750305
ISBN-10: 2491750309

HOLLAND HOUSE
ISBN-13: 9798856031323

ENCYCLOPOCALYPSE
ISBN-13: 9781959205845
ISBN-10: 1959205846

ECHO ON PUBLICATIONS
ISBN-13: 9781916582026
ISBN-10: 1916582028

ALSO BY CHRISTIAN FRANCIS

ALSO BY CHRISTIAN FRANCIS

ECHO ON PUBLICATIONS
ISBN-13: 9781916582095
ISBN-10: 1916582095

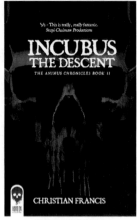

ECHO ON PUBLICATIONS
ISBN-13: 9781959205913
ISBN-10: 1959205919

ECHO ON PUBLICATIONS
ISBN-13: 9798386183592

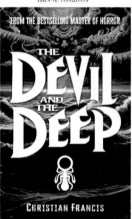

ECHO ON PUBLICATIONS
ISBN-13: 9781916582538
ISBN-10: 1916582532